T0207780

SARA INVESTIGATES

MAPLE LEAF RETIREMENT HOME MYSTERIES

S. L. MCGREGOR

iUniverse®

SARA INVESTIGATES
MAPLE LEAF RETIREMENT HOME MYSTERIES

iUniverse books may be ordered through booksellers or by contacting:

iUniverse
1663 Liberty Drive
Bloomington, IN 47403
www.iuniverse.com
844-349-9409

ISBN: 978-1-6632-3506-0 (sc)
ISBN: 978-1-6632-4171-9 (e)

Print information available on the last page.

iUniverse rev. date: 06/25/2022

DISCLAIMER

I do not condone murdering people or animals, just characters in a novel or short story.

Sara Investigates is a work of fiction. The characters herein are either composites of people I know now or people I have known in the past, or they are totally made up to accomplish a task necessary to the plot. The variety of activities and the delicious foods are real.

CONTENTS

MURDER ON THE TERRACE

This was the perfect move for me. I sat in my living room as I enjoyed my coffee while looking at my view of the CN Tower and the office buildings of downtown Toronto.

I had just recently moved into the Maple Leaf Retirement building after living for the past five years in an apartment in Scarborough. I was finding everything, especially the view, just perfect. My apartment was a lot smaller than I was used to, but it had amenities I'd never had before. In the bathroom I had a washer and dryer. No more going down to the laundry room with my coins and dirty laundry once a week.

In the kitchen I had a dishwasher, which seemed extravagant for one person, but I knew I would enjoy it.

I had brought my own furniture and electronics with me so that both Ryder, my 18-pound cat, and I could feel right at home.

I had had Ryder for almost 10 years. I found her in the barn on my parents' property and couldn't resist the cute little furball. Now, of course, that furball was huge and shed fur all over my furniture and the floor of my apartment. But I wouldn't give Ryder up now—she was a part of the family.

My other indulgence was my fish tank. I had always found tropical fish to be a calming, relaxing hobby, both pleasant to look after and enjoyable to watch as they swam around the tank. So there was a 10-gallon tropical fish tank in the living room for my and Ryder's enjoyment.

Some of my favourite eating places were just a short walk away.

Because I l now lived in downtown Toronto, the essential businesses were just a short cab ride away.

There was a pool across the road. I realized some places had a pool in the building, but I was never really into swimming, so this pool was close enough.

The elementary school next door would provide entertainment as I watched the children playing in the schoolyard. There was something calming about listening to children playing. From twelve floors up, even the screamers and screechers sounded pleasant. I might have felt differently if I lived on a lower floor, but from up here it was just fine.

The residents living on the other side of the building would hear the children on the soccer field and the track. There was also a skating rink, or what I was assuming would be made into a skating rink in the winter. For now, I could see the children Rollerblading on it.

This seemed like the ideal place to live out my retirement years after so many years of having worked at the hospital. I couldn't wait to get to know my neighbours. I was sure they would be as pleasant as my surroundings.

After getting myself ready for dinner, I went down to eat in the dining room and meet my new friends. After years of making my own meals, it was a pleasure to have someone else make the food and then do the dishes. I just had to go down to the ground level in the elevator and enjoy the food, along with the view of the park across the street and the witty conversations of my new friends.

I met up with Matthew, Donna and Joan. Matthew was a

tall, handsome man. He appeared to be a little older than I. He had that swagger that said, *I know I'm good-looking.*

Joan appeared to be about my age. She was a very pleasant Englishwoman.

Donna was a bubbly, very outgoing woman. She was wearing a short-sleeved T-shirt, and I could see her well-defined arm muscles and flat stomach. She looked as if she went to the gym every day. I would have to ask her about that. The gym was one of the reasons I had moved into this building.

I sat down with my new friends at their usual table and ordered the featured dinner—chicken parmesan. It was wonderful and, according to Joan, as delicious as usual.

The conversation during dinner was interesting. Joan was telling us about her day. She still worked part-time at a local shoe store. The stories she told us about the women trying to fit into shoes one or two sizes too small if the shoes they wanted didn't come in their size were both entertaining and sad.

I had the Nanaimo bar for dessert. Matthew had lemon meringue pie, and Donna had the fresh fruit.

Matthew told us about his day. He had spent a lot of the afternoon at the bar.

That wasn't my idea of a fun afternoon. I would prefer a cup of tea and pastries and sitting in the sunshine on a beautiful day like today had been.

Matthew seemed like a bit of a cad, but I was sure I could get along with him. I was positive I would develop a friendship with Donna and Joan.

I realized I had better start to get ready for the housewarming party on the terrace this evening. My tablemates, or my friends as I was starting to consider them, were going as well, so we all left dinner with a friendly "See you in a bit."

A little later, I got out of the elevator on the ninth floor.

Stepping outside onto the terrace, I took a look around at the beautiful view. Seeing my new friend Donna starting to put out the hors d'oeuvres, I went over to help her. We set up the fresh fruit platter with melon chunks on picks, as well as a large shrimp platter and a dessert tray with squares and cookies for those who preferred sweets.

"Did you hear Carmen and George yelling at each other this afternoon?" Donna asked me. Even in my short time living there, I knew that Carmen was a bossy woman who lived on my floor.

"Yes, I did," I replied. "I was surprised to hear George so angry. He is usually very quiet. I was in Louise's apartment just beside George's apartment, so I heard the whole thing,George was extremely angry that Carmen had taken apartment 1255. It has the best view and the most closet space. He tried to get it when he signed up for an apartment months ago, but Carmen insisted that she had gotten that one when she put her deposit down. George was insisting that she give up her apartment to him. I've never heard him so angry," I added.

I was needed at the drinks table, so I moved on.

As I had helped Donna put out the hors d'oeuvres, I couldn't help but notice our chef, Michael, had outdone himself. Donna and I stood back to admire Michael's creations. "I'm sure they will taste as good as they look," Donna said just before she screamed. As I started to walk towards her, I looked over at her. She appeared terrified. She was pointing at something behind the table. From where I was standing, it looked like a pile of clothes.

"What is that behind the table?" I asked Donna. She was unable to answer. She just kept pointing at the pile of clothes. I continued to walk over to the table. As I got closer, I could see that it was Carmen. It looked as if she had been hit over the head with a patio umbrella. I pulled out my cell phone and called 9-1-1. I had to look away from Carmen. I now understood Donna's reaction. I was speechless as well.

When the 9-1-1 operator answered, I managed to let her know what I had seen. At least I hoped my response to the operator was coherent enough for her to understand. Then Donna and I both moved away from the table and waited for the police to arrive. Talking to the operator had calmed us both sufficiently enough that we could speak.

"I have never seen a dead body before," Donna told me in a trembling voice.

As we put our arms around each other, I replied, "I hope she's not dead." I had never seen a dead body either. This was very upsetting.

The police showed up before the guests started to arrive. Donna and I answered their questions as best as we could. Unfortunately, we weren't much help, both of us having been so focused on the food and how best to display it that we hadn't noticed anything or anyone unusual on the terrace.

After the questioning was finished, Donna and I both went back to our respective apartments. I don't know about Donna, but I had a lavender tea when I got back to my apartment, and tried my best to ignore Ryder, my 18-pound cat, who was trying to convince me she was starving.

The next morning, I got a visit from Kevin Hanson, the detective in charge. Detective Hanson was a good-looking man about my age. He was wearing a suit and tie, but I could see that he was very muscular under that suit. He had short salt-and-pepper hair and eyes that looked determined but caring with just a slight twinkle to them. However, the one feature that really caught my eye was his crooked smile. I wasn't sure why, but I had always been attracted to men with a crooked smile. I invited him into my apartment.

I was definitely attracted to Detective Hanson and was willing to help out with this case in any way I could. By this time, I was a little calmer and better able to answer his questions. He told me that they had checked the cameras for this building and no one had entered the building yesterday afternoon. It had to be someone from this residence who was the culprit. I supposed that should have scared me, and it did, but at the time I was thinking, *This guy is quite good-looking.*

Later, at dinnertime, I sat with Paul at his table. Paul was a very interesting older man who originally had come from Vietnam. He told me that Carmen and Ray had gone to dinner last week and Carmen's boyfriend Matthew was very angry about it. Paul could hear Matthew threatening Carmen with what he would do if she ever had dinner with another guy again. Paul said that Matthew was very loud and the language he had used was not very civil at all. Something that Paul was not used to hearing, apparently. Paul did strike me as someone who would never lose his temper over something so insignificant.

Later that evening I thought about what Paul had told me. Ray was an older man who was definitely not looking for a woman as a companion. The two of them probably had just met in the hall and, rather than eat alone, just sat down together. It didn't have to mean anything. Why would Matthew be so angry? I would have to ask Donna her opinion tomorrow.

The next day I met Donna in the gym. As we raced on our stationary bicycles, I asked her about Matthew and Carmen. Apparently, Carmen had been trying to find someone else. She didn't like Matthew's volatile temper.

Donna thought Carmen and George were a new couple before Carmen's death.

That was interesting gossip, well worth getting up for at seven o'clock in the morning and racing on a stationary bike for 30 minutes. Donna won our race. She managed to go 15 kilometres in 30 minutes, whereas I was only able to do 10 kilometres.

Later that afternoon, I met up with my friend Jaime. She had a cockapoo named Buttons. It was a miserable dog.

Earlier today, I had agreed to meet Jaime at the Creamery King at four in the afternoon. She knew some of the people in this building. I thought I would ask her about Matthew. I didn't get to the CK very often, so it was a treat for me, except that I had to tolerate my friend's cockapoo. Buttons snapped at my heels the whole time Jaime and I were talking. It made it difficult to enjoy a cookie dough ice cream sundae—not impossible, but difficult.

Jaime lived across the street from my building. I had tried to get into that building, but there were no vacancies when I was looking, so I ended up at the Maple Leaf—a decision I so far hadn't regretted.

After the usual gossip about the people we used to work with, Jaime told me some new gossip I hadn't heard about this building. She was going to move into my building and was given apartment 1155. She was very excited about the apartment and the view. It faced east, so she would be able to see the Don Valley and the Beaches. The person currently living there was moving to an available apartment in my building, so his unit would be available soon. Jaime was going to move in by the end of the month.

"Then we can meet every day for coffee when I take Buttons for his walk."

Oh, yay. So I guessed George was moving into Carmen's apartment. He sure hadn't lost any time.

The next morning, I was walking through the lobby, on my way to the drugstore a few blocks away—easy to get to when I needed some supplies. I noticed George talking with Fred. I asked them if either of them wanted to go with me as it was such a nice day. George mentioned that he also needed some supplies and would walk with me. As we passed a mail truck picking up the letters from the mailbox on the corner, George started reminiscing about his career at the Mississauga Canada Post depot. I found out he still maintained friendships he had developed during his 30-year career. In fact, a group of them had gotten together the previous Saturday night for dinner and drinks at Ruth Chris here in downtown Toronto.

When I got back to the Maple Leaf, as I was picking up my mail in the main lobby, I ran into Matthew—not literally of course, but I stopped to chat. Matthew was concerned because Renee was going to Wanda's to get a coffee. Renee was an older resident who was starting to have difficulty remembering things. "We can't let her pester the cashier for a free coffee. If she keeps this up, they won't let us in the restaurant—and I like the single burgers with fries," he told me.

Donna came in. "I like the chicken pecan salad." No wonder she regularly beat me in our bicycle races.

I agreed to walk with Renee to Wanda's. *What the heck? I might as well get a strawberry frosted ice cream.*

On the way, I noticed that Renee was wearing two different shoes—a running shoe and a dress shoe with a heel. No wonder she was complaining about the limp she seemed to have today. Seeing as she was older, she usually had someone come in to help her get dressed. Apparently today that person hadn't shown up.

On our way up to Dundas Street, we passed the Italian restaurant that would soon open.

Renee used to live in Rosedale and liked everyone to know it. Why not? I probably would too if I had lived in such a beautiful neighbourhood. I was not ashamed that I lived in Scarborough. It was a warm and friendly neighbourhood. But I did notice for someone from such a rich neighbourhood, she always seemed to be short of money. Today was no exception. She didn't have enough to buy her double burger, so I bought her one, as well as some fries. Maybe she was just cheap, but if she did need some food, I was happy to help. With me to pay for her coffee, Renee didn't give the cashier a hassle about charging her for it. The job of a cashier in this neighbourhood couldn't be easy, but they each always gave us a big smile.

As we walked home from Wanda's, Renee told me all about the large house she owned in Rosedale. It sounded opulent. I asked her if her son was coming to visit her soon. Apparently, he was too busy at work to drop by one evening to visit his mother. Part of me couldn't blame him—she was not a nice woman—but she was his mother. As I contemplated this, I looked down the street and saw Jaime coming with Buttons.

How often does that thing need to be walked?

Thinking that a person shouldn't have to tolerate both Renee and Buttons in one walk, I turned at the corner to go into the building through the back door. This confused Renee, who was one to get confused easily. I told her that it was such a nice day that we would stay outside longer. It also gave me a chance to ask her more about her son.

The next afternoon at three o'clock, we had our body balance exercise class. A lot of people showed up to this class because at our age, balance was very important, so anything that helped us with that was appreciated. I got dressed in my exercise clothes and shoes and headed to the ninth floor, where the class was held. I tried to get there early, but Donna beat me to the class. She was very gung-ho about exercising. She was talking to Mike. Mike and his wife, Claire, were members of many of the committees here at the Maple Leaf. Donna and Mike seemed to be having a very serious discussion. I hoped she wouldn't forget about the class.

I got through this class with less effort than it had taken the first time I tried it. My daily exercising helped with this. At the end of the class, Donna pulled me aside and said she wanted to talk to me. It was a nice day, so we went to the terrace. Donna said, "Mike told me that Renee's son works at Canada Post in Mississauga. He used to work with George many years ago. He told Renee that George is an upright kind of guy who never got involved with the other workers at the Canada Post depot." I asked Donna if she believed this story.

She answered, "I don't think Mike would lie to me, so I believe that someone told him that."

I didn't believe this for two reasons. One was that it would be very difficult to work somewhere for any length of time without getting involved with one's co-workers, even if it was just a superficial relationship during work hours. The second was that George had told me a group from Canada Post had gotten together the previous Saturday for dinner. How would he know if he hadn't been included?

I expressed my misgivings to Donna. She said, "I agree. I just wanted to find out what you thought about it."

Back in my apartment, I told Ryder this latest gossip. She just meowed and looked bored. I couldn't blame her. I wasn't sure if I believed what I'd been told about George. I agreed with Donna. I believed Mike. Something made me feel uneasy about this piece of gossip. Why would Renee's son mention George to Renee? I was sure Renee did not know George.

A few of the women in my building had decided to go to the community pool across the street. I'd never been to it, but these women, who liked to swim, had.

This left our knitting club very small today. It was just me and three other women who were also unable to swim. In the knitting club, everyone knit their own projects but shared their gossip. I was working on knitting a blanket to give to a local mission on Spadina Avenue. But today, my main reason for being there was to find out what the others knew about Renee. I had known Renee wouldn't be at the knitting club meeting. No food was usually served at this activity, so Renee didn't come.

Louise was there. She was the closest friend Renee had in this building, if Renee could be said to have any friends. With her brash manner and inability to remember things, Renee hadn't made many friends since moving here. Louise told me that Renee was unable to sell her house and was very short on cash, adding that Renee regularly spoke about a big payoff that was coming. Louise wasn't sure when, but she said it sounded like it would happen soon.

After our meeting, I went down to the main lobby to get my mail. Donald, the handsome concierge, was there, so I asked him about recent visitors to the building.

According to Donald's information, Renee was mistaken. Her son had visited several times over the past few weeks. I was both relieved and concerned—relieved because her son did seem to care about her, but concerned because it seemed she was trying to keep her son's visit a secret. This made me wonder what her reason could be. Or perhaps she had forgotten that her son had been here several times recently. If that were the case, then she was getting worse. I didn't want to think about that.

Instead, I picked up my mail, which consisted of grocery store flyers and the usual hardware store flyers. If I hadn't stopped to talk to Donald, this trip would have been a complete waste of time.

When I got back to my apartment, I went through the flyers to pick out this week's treats. *Oh yay! Kitty litter is on sale.* When you are an 18-pound cat, you go through a lot of kitty litter. I looked up and saw Ryder sitting on top of the fish tank. "Ryder, get off that aquarium. You are scaring the fish to death," I said to the indifferent cat. What had I been thinking getting both a cat and fish?

I thought it might help me to determine who the murderer was if I could hear what others in the building were saying about this murder. Did anyone have more details about it than they should have?

Not being an expert at this surveillance thing, I got a newspaper and sat in the lobby reading it. The only thing a little less obvious would be if I were wearing a fake nose and mustache, so I thought I would give it a try. It could work.

I sat there for quite a while reading the newspaper, but no one came into the lobby. I waited some more. Then a group of women came in and sat in the adjacent chairs. I peeked over the top of my newspaper. "Hi, Sara!" Janice yelled out. So much for hiding behind a newspaper. I decided to talk with these women. I figured I might as well; everyone in the lobby now knew I was there, and I was tired of reading *The Star*'s complaints of Justin Trudeau's government.

This group of women had heard of Carmen's death but didn't know any details. No one seemed upset about the murder, but they commented that they would miss her at the book club meetings. Carmen was very opinionated and kept the conversation going, so if someone hadn't quite finished the book and had nothing to say, it wasn't obvious. Carmen usually dominated the discussion anyway. I was glad to hear that the book club would miss her.

I asked Thelma about her new granddaughter, and that kept the discussion going until some other people came into the lobby.

Matthew, George and Ray came in a group into the lobby. They were on their way to the Empire Pub, which dated back to 1867. In my opinion, they had the best fish and chips in the area. I decided to join the guys and see if any of them knew about the murder.

When we got to the pub, we sat at their usual table, which gave us a really nice view of the architecture of the old building. The walls were wood with big wooden beams along the walls and ceiling.

After placing our orders of fish and chips, I asked Matthew if he had heard any news lately. He saw right through my casual inquiry. In addition to being handsome, Matthew was one of the most intelligent men in the building.

He said, "I heard that it was Carmen who was killed. I didn't like Carmen at all. We knew each other prior to moving into the Maple Leaf, and I didn't like her then either. She was very rude and rubbed me the wrong way."

Thinking this was a little harsh to say about someone who had just died, I told Matthew, "There must have been something positive about her. Do you know if she had any friends here?"

George jumped in at this point. "It wasn't a natural death. She deserved it," he said in an angry tone.

I thought this sounded a little unforgiving to say even if one didn't like the person.

Ray knew when and where it happened. He mentioned that he thought she was an interesting person and had wanted to get to know her better. He said, "She must have had a lot of money because she had just recently sold her house in Scarborough. I would like to have become friends with her."

Now that was a very mercenary reaction.

"Did no one like her as a person?" I asked.

There was silence from the group. I had gotten my answer.

I asked Ray how he knew so many details of Carmen's death. He said, "Donna told me the details."

I found that hard to believe. We had been asked—no, told—not to discuss any details with anyone until after the investigation was over. I had just met Donna when I moved in here recently, but she struck me as the type of person to follow the rules. However, I had found out something: I hadn't known before this that Carmen had recently sold her house. I would have to check into that. Maybe I was wrong about the motive and the person who did it.

We finished our lunches and then decided to walk back to the Maple Leaf. It was such a warm sunny day, and it wasn't too far of a walk.

On the way home, Matthew told us about the buildings in this neighbourhood. Most of them had been here for many years, but there were a few new ones. Matthew pointed out the new TD Bank that had just opened up near our building.

I mentioned, "It is very handy to have a bank within walking distance."

George said, "I didn't realize the bank was open yet."

Matthew flew into a rage and started yelling at him,

accusing him of lying. "You used the ATM at this bank just last week to get money for our lunch."

George was adamant that the money for last week's lunch at the Empire had come from a different bank. "I wasn't aware that this bank existed," George asserted.

Matthew was equally sure that it was this bank that George had used. I tried to add that it didn't really matter, saying, "We now know the bank is here." But both men were unyielding in their opinion of which bank George had used. I headed back to the Maple Leaf.

Donna was in the lobby when I got there. I could talk to her about what Ray had said.

"No, I never mentioned any of the details to anyone, especially not Ray. I think he is a little creepy. Maybe he was listening in while we were talking with the detective. I've noticed Ray hanging around doorways, probably listening to other people's conversations, before," Donna told me in response to my question.

Oh great, I thought. *Another person I need to be concerned about.* Or maybe it was just one person.

Back at my apartment, I opened my window and listened. I couldn't hear Matthew yelling, which surprised me. He had been yelling pretty loudly when I left him with George. I saw them from my window still standing on the sidewalk, I assume arguing about which bank they had gone to last week. I smiled as I thought, *Wouldn't one of them have a receipt from their transaction?*

Men! I thought as I made myself a tea and pulled out some cookies to have a relaxing afternoon reading the latest edition of the *Maple Leaf Gazette*, a monthly newsletter that included news, residents' stories and word games. I was finding this newsletter very informative, and the word games helped to keep my mind active.

The next morning after breakfast I decided to skip the exercises and just go to the terrace. It was such a beautiful sunny day that I decided I would take my coffee and newspaper and enjoy the fresh air. I sat down at a table and opened the newspaper to the puzzle section, thinking I had had enough of bad news this week. It was time for fun. As I was trying to figure out the second puzzle, I looked up. There on his balcony was Matthew. I gave him a friendly wave, but he didn't wave back. Instead, he started to yell at me.

"I could kill you. You've started a rumour that I killed Carmen, and now Elaine refuses to see me anymore. I thought we had the start of something special. Now she is sitting in the dining room with Larry."

I started to call back to him that I never started that rumour, but he had already gone back into his apartment.

So much for my relaxing morning. I guess I will continue the puzzles in my apartment. I didn't know where he'd gotten the idea that I started that rumour.

The next morning, I wanted to see if George was watching the bank in the mornings. There must have been a reason for him to lie about not using it. I snuck out of the building early with my binoculars. If anyone were to ask, I could say I was going birdwatching. Okay, maybe birds weren't out this early, but you never know.

Noticing the van arriving at the bank, I took out my binoculars. I checked out the windows of my building and saw George watching the bank with his binoculars.

That afternoon I had a knock at my door. I was in the middle of playing a game of solitaire on my computer. Talking to a real person would have been preferable, although I wasn't sure Ryder would agree. She sat beside my computer and batted at the screen when I moved the cards. So, I guessed technically it was not solitaire if the two of us were playing. But I digress.

I was surprised to find Larry at my door. He had never visited me before.

Larry told me that he had overheard Matthew and George arguing the other day. He said that he actually had seen George at the new bank about a week ago. He asked me to let Matthew know.

"Both Matthew and George have really bad tempers. I'm actually a little afraid of them. But you seem to be friends with them, so you could let Matthew know," he said to me.

Larry then went on to let me know that he believed George was just mistaken. "I used to work with George at the Canada Post facility in Mississauga," he said. "George is an honest person, but he does anger easily."

After Larry left, as I thought about our conversation, I concluded that something didn't seem right. Why had he wanted me to know that George was honest? I would have to talk with Larry again.

That evening after a delicious dinner of fish and pasta that I made in my toaster oven, I decided to go to the bistro for a while and do my dishes later. Most Friday evenings there was a crowd of people in the bistro. We could buy cold drinks or coffee and some crudités there. The conversation was usually lively and loud. When I got there, William met me at the door carrying my favourite drink—a large latte. Awhile later, I thought the evening was going well, but then William pulled me aside and said in a firm voice, "You'd better stop investigating this murder. It could be very dangerous for you if you don't." Based on his tone, I wasn't sure it was just a friendly warning from a concerned friend. I asked him how he knew about the investigation. "I was talking with George earlier. He told me that you are asking a lot of questions about this murder. The police aren't asking about it, so you should stop being such a nuisance."

Okay, I'd gotten my answer. It wasn't a friendly warning.

Later that evening as I was preparing to leave the bistro, William's partner, Lewis, grabbed my arm to stop me and said, "Please don't worry about William. He is stressed right now because we are having financial difficulties. William has assured me they will be resolved soon, but in the meantime, he is acting very strangely, even for him."

Monday morning, I woke up at my usual early hour and went to the gym to use the treadmill. As I was looking out the window enjoying the view of the skyline, it dawned on me: *The gym is just three floors below Carmen's apartment.* While I was contemplating that disturbing thought, I noticed that I was able to see the back door of the bank across the street. I could see that the Brinks truck was making a delivery. Could someone have wanted Carmen's apartment in order to know exactly when the bank would have the most money?

Every Monday morning a group of us got together in the lounge for a coffee and some gossip. I usually tried to go to the lounge for this event in order to keep in touch with my friends and get coffee and conversation without having to deal with Buttons snapping at my heels. Today I brewed my coffee while getting ready to go down to the ninth floor to meet my friends.

I thought that this week it would be especially important to go. As far as I knew, Donna and I were the only ones who knew who the victim was. I might hear something.

Boy, was I naive. It seemed everyone knew more than I did. I started to ask around and got some interesting answers.

Charlene told me that Carmen hadn't made many friends. She was so bossy and demanding that no one could tolerate her.

Elaine was not there. I asked Rhonda about Elaine because she was usually at these get-togethers. "I haven't seen Elaine for a few days, ever since Matthew's yelling match with her. She has been keeping a low profile. Now that I think about it, I haven't seen her at all for a few days." Rhonda sounded concerned.

"I hope she's okay." I made a mental note to myself to email Elaine.

Rhonda asked around and learned that no one else remembered seeing Elaine for a few days.

There had been one thing bothering me for the last few days, even more than if I should get a raised maple or chocolate doughnut with my coffee. It seemed like a lot of trouble just to make sure one didn't lose some of the money. There wouldn't be a lot of people in this neighbourhood who used the bank first thing in the morning. So why did George need a good view of the bank? I had seen George watching for the bank truck a few mornings ago. He knew the money got delivered every day prior to opening time. Did it really matter if some of the money had been disbursed and he didn't get the full delivery? Maybe I was wrong about who murdered Carmen and why they had done it. Of course, that wouldn't answer the question of why George had been looking at the bank through binoculars.

I decided that tomorrow morning I would go to the bank even before my coffee to check it out.

The next morning, I left the Maple Leaf early and crossed the road. As I had planned, I got to the bank before it was open. I stood by the front door, trying to look like I was waiting for the bank to open, but I was keeping an eye on the bank security guard who was waiting on the other side of the door. He came over to me and told me I would have to leave. He was very polite about it but very forceful. He said, "The Brinks truck will be here soon. After they leave, the bank will be open and you can go inside. In the meantime, maybe you can go to the coffee shop just over there." He pointed to the Maple Leaf Espresso, then gently took my arm and escorted me off the property. I apologized and advised him that I would be back later in the day, after my coffee and doughnut.

I thought I had gotten my answer regarding why George had to be at the bank exactly when the truck arrived. The truck contained the money, which would soon be securely locked in the vault. I figured I may even deserve an apple fritter with my coffee today. I headed back to the Maple Leaf. Perhaps I didn't need a latte this early in the morning.

Later, as I sat drinking my latte outside the Maple Leaf Espresso, my neighbour's dog sniffed at my leg. Luckily, my neighbour came along and shooed him away before he could do anything else. I definitely didn't need that today. I was going to see Detective Handsome to give him my theory. If I could help to solve this murder, maybe he would notice me.

Charlene sat down with a mocha and a delicious-smelling slice of gingerbread. "You will never believe what I heard last night" was the first thing she said before she even got a bite of her gingerbread.

I knew this gossip would be tasty.

"Matthew was yelling and screaming at Louise, saying he will kill her if she doesn't stop eating in the dining room with Jackson. If I were Louise, I would take him seriously. He has a temper," Charlene said.

Well, there goes my theory. Maybe it was Matthew. I can't go to Detective Handsome with two ideas. I'm glad I didn't make an appointment to meet with him. I will have to investigate some more.

My day was just about to get very exciting.

After talking with Charlene for a while, I went to look for Matthew, sure he could explain his behaviour towards Carla. It took me awhile, but eventually I found him on the terrace.

"Did you threaten Louise?" I asked him.

"Yes I did, but I didn't mean it," he said. "I apologized to her. I'm so embarrassed that I let the issue get to me. It doesn't matter who she eats with," he added.

I was very relieved.

Later, I got back to my apartment. Sitting down with a cup of hot chocolate would be perfect right now, but as I prepared to do just that, I noticed my cat, Ryder, sitting on top of my aquarium, looking as proud as a cat that had just captured a 10-gallon tank could be. I got her some treats, and she reluctantly accepted them. I then looked out the window and noticed Jack and Parker on their bikes riding towards the park. Earlier I had noticed Alice and Stan going to the park. These two couples didn't usually get together. *I'm going to go check this out,* I told myself.

When I finally got to the park, Alice and Stan were just leaving. Parker told me that Alice had told him that she saw Clara leaving the terrace just before the party was supposed to start. Clara seemed very flustered and upset. She hadn't been seen in her usual classes since then. Clara was a 100-pound, 95-year-old woman. I couldn't imagine her lifting one of the patio umbrellas, much less hitting someone with one hard enough to kill them. But stranger things have happened.

While I was out, I thought I would get myself a treat and then head up to the terrace to see if it was open yet. *The police should be finished their investigation by now,* I thought.

I decided on a strawberry ice cream and headed to the ninth floor. The police were just finishing up and let me onto the terrace. Detective Hanson (I'd come to think of him as Detective Handsome) told me that the patio umbrella wasn't the murder weapon. It had been just placed there to make it look like it was. The murder weapon was a rock in the garden that was then replaced. It was not very big, but with some strength it was able to do the job.

Okay, so now I knew it wasn't Clara who'd done it. She may have disliked Carmen, but she didn't have the strength to do this. I would need to find her and try to find out if she knew anything.

The next morning, I slept in a little late and read the paper with my breakfast before going to the gym to ride the bike. In the paper I noticed an interesting article about a bank robbery at a bank on the west side of the city. Somehow, the bank robbers seemed to know when the bank was receiving its supply of money and struck just as the truck was arriving. Luckily, no one had been hurt during the robbery.

I finished my coffee, put on my exercise clothes and headed for the gym. The bike was already busy, so I used the treadmill. I was looking out the window enjoying the view when Joan came in.

Joan could find something to complain about with everything. She was busy complaining about how hot and sunny it had been lately.

I continued looking out the window at the beautiful day, trying not to pay attention to Joan. The bank did not have a delivery this morning. I guessed they didn't get deliveries every day.

Having made up my mind that I had this figured out, I

called Detective Handsome and asked him to meet me. He was able to meet later that morning.

To fill in the time, I texted Jaime to ask if she wanted to meet. She agreed to meet me at the Maple Leaf Espresso. After meeting with Jaime and Buttons, I didn't have a lot of time to get ready for Detective Handsome.

I only had time enough to quickly go up to my apartment and change my shoes and put on some lipstick. Then I rushed over to the park, where I sat down on the bench and tried to organize my thoughts and figure out the best way to present my idea without sounding critical of the way the detective was handling the investigation. Handsome's team was doing a great job with this investigation, but in the short time I had been in this building, I had gotten to know some of the residents and their unique personalities. One couldn't do that in a 20-minute interview. I hoped Detective Handsome would view me as helpful, not critical—the last thing I wanted to be.

As I sat there waiting, I watched the children playing soccer in the middle of the field. Along the outside of the soccer field there was a track and a few children running around it. In the soccer field there were young children learning to kick the ball. I watched as someone held the ball and one little guy ran up and kicked. He looked amazed that the ball had moved. It was fun to watch.

Then Detective Handsome came and sat down on the bench beside me. I thought cops always drank coffee and ate doughnuts, but Detective Handsome hadn't brought anything to this meeting. And honestly, he looked as if he'd never eaten a doughnut in his life. He was very muscular. But I digress.

"I have figured out who killed Carmen!" I blurted out.

He looked surprised, so I told him my theory. After I'd told him all the details, he looked at me as if I were crazy. And I was beginning to think I was. Maybe I should have worked out a few more of the details before talking to him.

Kevin said in a neutral tone, "I assure you, we have a team of professional detectives working on this case, and everyone at the Maple Leaf, including you, should not be worried about your safety."

I felt sufficiently dismissed, so I took a walk around the block, stopping, of course, at the Maple Leaf Espresso coffee shop to console my bruised ego.

The morning after my appointment with Detective Handsome, I went to meet my favourite couple, Bob and Doug, on the terrace. They were both so positive and charming that they could help me get over the disappointment of my meeting yesterday. They had both just gotten back from a bike ride along the Don Valley. Doug mentioned how beautiful and green the leaves were right now. I told them about my meeting with Kevin and my theory about how the murder happened. They both agreed that my theory could have some merit, but they weren't sure. Oh well, at least I didn't leave feeling stupid. I would have to work some more on my idea. Maybe Matthew would be a good person to talk with next. But before I could do that, I had a fish tank that needed cleaning.

I went back to my apartment and changed into sweatpants and a grubby T-shirt in preparation for cleaning the aquarium. I was just about to start to clean the tank—a messy but necessary job—when Detective Handsome called to say he wanted to talk to me. He would be there in thirty minutes. *Oh my goodness, I will have to clean out the kitty litter and change my clothes. Oh, and put on some lipstick. The fish will have to wait until later.*

I had just finished getting dressed when there was a knock at the door. It was Handsome with two coffees.

He said, "I wanted to talk in person to apologize for my

reaction yesterday. Your theory definitely has merit. I'm just not convinced it was necessary to kill Carmen to execute the plan. There definitely is a gang robbing banks across Toronto."

"I agree. I can't understand why murder was part of the plan either. Maybe I am wrong about who did it. She wasn't a well-liked person. Maybe it was personal," I admitted.

We finished our coffees and talked about hobbies. Handsome played pickleball with his co-workers in his spare time. One thing we did have in common was our taste in music. He also liked opera music, and my favourite, *La bohème,* was his favourite opera as well. We both reminisced about going to the O'Keefe Centre, as it was called back then, to see this opera with our respective spouses. That led to a discussion of our current situations. Handsome's wife had been gone for more than ten years now. My husband died five years ago. We talked about how difficult the last few years had been. Then Detective Handsome got a phone call and had to leave. Oh well, I needed to get back to my fish tank anyway.

The next morning, I got up early and went to the gym as usual to walk on the treadmill. This case was certainly helping me with my fitness goal. As I was looking out the window towards the bank, I saw the truck pull up to deliver the money. Right away I saw a man cross the road and go over to the delivery truck. He pulled a gun on the delivery man, snatched up several bundles of money, put them in his knapsack, then ran towards our building. Now I could clearly see his face, but of course he didn't see me watching him from the ninth floor. It looked like … yes, it was! It was George. I immediately phoned Kevin, the handsome detective, but of course it was too early for him to be in the office. I left a message to let him know what I was about to do.

I immediately went to the 12th floor to apartment 1265.

George took his time answering—probably stashing the money away so I wouldn't see it. This gave me a chance to cool down, but not much. It also give me a chance to figure out why George needed this apartment. He needed a clear view of the bank yard and the ability it gave him to get to the bank quickly without being seen. If he got to the bank too early, the bank guard would send him away. If he got there too late, the money would be locked in the vault.

When George finally answered the door, I blurted out, "I saw you at the bank. Is that why you murdered Carmen, to get this apartment?"

George's rage grew by the second. I could see it on his face. He grabbed me. As I struggled, he started to drag me towards the garbage room down the hall. It was difficult for me to keep my balance. Maybe this wasn't such a good idea after all.

"George, Carmen was a good friend. Why was it necessary to kill her?" I managed to ask.

"Because she wouldn't mind her own business. She had to keep questioning why I wanted that apartment. I had to kill her to keep her quiet. And now I have to kill you for the same reason," he said, growling at me.

I managed to grab the door to the garbage room and hang on. George kept pulling me towards the garbage chute. Seeing that I was losing my grip on the door frame, I dried to dig my nails into it but was unable. Then, I heard the elevator opening and started to shout. George hit me so hard that I was sure something was broken. As he opened the door to the garbage chute, I heard Kevin's voice. "Help me!" I cried out, before George covered my mouth. Just then, my handsome detective came in and pulled me away from the garbage chute and out of the garbage room before putting handcuffs on George.

Handsome's backup arrived and read George his rights before taking him away.

"I will be right with you guys," Handsome said to his backup, then turned to me and with a serious face. "Why didn't you wait for me? George wasn't going anywhere."

I had no answer, so instead I smiled and, unbeknown to Handsome, just melted inside.

MURDER IN THE FAMILY

One fall afternoon, there was a knock at my door. When I answered it, I discovered my friend Donna standing there. I invited her in.

"Sara, there is an opening on the Welcoming Committee. You would be great on that committee," the well-intentioned Donna mentioned.

I guess that she'd forgotten that I very briefly used to belong to one of the committees here at the Maple Leaf. It was not a pleasant experience for me. But this one sounded a lot more positive, and if it would give me a chance to help new residents feel welcome and a little less confused about where things were and how to get things done, I was happy to help. I remembered when I first moved in, it was very confusing. Although the dining room didn't have assigned seats, people had gotten used to sitting in the same spots, so it was a challenge for me to find a table at dinner without upsetting several residents. If I could help someone with this, I would be happy.

"Okay, I will join the committee. Where is the form to sign?" I asked as she was handing it to me.

I thought I should be suspicious about her eagerness to get me on the committee, but she was a good friend and I trusted her. As she was leaving my apartment with the signed form, she mentioned, "I will take the form down right away. The committee meets this evening at seven in the boardroom."

"See you there," I said as she closed the door.

The Maple Leaf Retirement Community had many positive activities. That was one of the reasons I had moved in here. Some of the people here, however, were a bit of a challenge. Karen, the head of the Welcoming Committee, was one of those challenging people. I had worked with her briefly on another committee. She was very controlling and didn't let the other members have a say.

I discussed my concerns with Ryder, my 18-pound cat, who didn't seem too concerned about my problem. She seemed more concerned about when her dinner would be served. I gave up on trying to get sympathy from a cat and started to prepare her dinner.

After getting Ryder her dinner, I got myself ready and went down to meet my friends Matthew, Donna and Joan. Tonight's featured dinner was trout with jasmine rice—two of my favourites. The conversation was witty as usual. Matthew talked about the local tour he had given that afternoon. They had gone to the distillery district and saw the beautiful 19th-century architecture of the breweries and pubs that were a big part of Toronto's history.

I said to Matthew, "I always thought that Toronto had the nickname Toronto the Good because they didn't allow alcohol consumption in the history of the city."

Matthew replied, "No, that is not the case. Molson's has a long history in Toronto."

"Of course. How could I have forgotten? I used to work for a company owned by Molson's."

By mentioning this, it seemed to prompt Joan to start talking about her current job working part-time at a local shoe store, Smith's Shoes. I thought it was wonderful that she got out and talked with other people. It gave her something to talk about with us at dinner. I found it interesting to hear about other people's workplaces.

Rather than eating my meal quickly, I enjoyed the main course. Then I skipped dessert in order to get to the meeting on time.

As I was leaving dinner to go to the Welcoming Committee meeting, I asked Donna, "Will I see you in the boardroom, or should I wait for you and we can go in together?"

"Oh no, I wouldn't go to that committee meeting if you paid me!" she exclaimed. "Karen heads up that committee!"

So much for trusting my friends. I guessed Donna had worked on one of Karen's committees before.

I got to the boardroom with, I thought, five minutes to spare. Karen glared at me and announced to the other attendees, "I'm glad we're *finally* all here. We can begin." During the meeting I found out that there were six new residents who would be moving in over the next week. *Yay!* Karen assigned who would be responsible for each one.

The committee consisted of Karen, who was the chair, and five other members including me. Louise was one of the original residents here. She was quiet; I was surprised to see her on the committee. Maybe she saw it as a way to meet other people.

Malcolm was an extrovert who didn't usually hide his feelings about a topic or refrain from giving his opinion.

John was a very friendly outgoing person who was always trying to help people.

Janet was a relatively new resident who would probably use the information she learned from this committee to help herself get oriented.

The mixture of personalities and experience on this committee would make us stronger. The only thing we had in common was our fear of Karen.

"There is one new resident moving in tomorrow. I will welcome him because he is a VIP. He was the CEO of the Port Perry Zoo prior to his retirement," Karen told us. She continued, saying, "His name is Thomas, and he's moving into apartment 755. Please do not bother him or his family, who will be here to help him move in tomorrow."

Next there was Faith, who was moving onto the 12th floor—probably Carmen's apartment. She had been a government employee in what sounded like an interesting position before her retirement. I thought she would be a great addition to our knitting group. I hoped she knit. John was responsible for welcoming her.

Then they talked about my friend Jaime who had moved in a week ago. Louisa was responsible for welcoming her.

There was also a new couple who had moved in yesterday. Maria was going to welcome them.

The final new resident we talked about was a gentleman named Jacob who had just retired from a career as an engineer. I thought my friend Matthew might be interested in talking with him. Matthew had been a carpenter before his retirement, so they might have a lot in common. Paul was given the task of welcoming Jacob.

I was not assigned a new resident, but I wouldn't give up on this committee. I would give it a few more tries. I believed the committee met monthly, so it wasn't too bad.

I got up extra early the next morning to try to beat Donna to the gym. Maybe the bike she always used was extra fast. By the time I got Ryder fed and myself dressed and to the gym,

Donna was already there, sitting on her usual bike. We did our half-hour race as usual, which Donna won.

Donna and I then went to the Maple Leaf Espresso for breakfast and coffee. I couldn't stay annoyed at Donna. I had been introduced to some new residents through the Welcoming Committee, and that was a good thing. Donna confessed that she had been selected to be on the Welcoming Committee and the only way Karen would let her out of her commitment was if she were to find a replacement. I had to admire Donna's deviousness. I wished I could do the same thing to someone else.

On my way back to my apartment from the gym, I happened to go past apartment 755 and see some people moving in. This was obviously Thomas's family. I knew we had all been told to stay away from this family, but I was here, so I thought I would go and see if they needed any help. I introduced myself. They seemed like a very nice family and seemed to be very organized. I liked that.

Thomas was sitting on the bed. An older gentleman, he was very well-dressed. He was directing the movers where to put each box.

The woman I assumed was Thomas's daughter was tall and thin with short curly blonde hair. She was dressed in a very expensive-looking stylish pantsuit. As I was introducing myself and telling her about the Maple Leaf, she was busy unpacking boxes and putting things away.

Thomas's daughter, who said her name was Corrine, introduced me to her son, Timothy.

Timothy was not helping with this move at all. In fact, he seemed to resent his grandfather. I wondered why he was there.

Malcolm came by and introduced himself. They were making arrangements to meet in the dining room, so I thought it would be a great time to slip away. I would try to meet up with Malcolm later at lunch to get his opinion of the committee.

At lunch, I found Malcolm at his usual table. The new resident was sitting with him, so I just stopped at his table briefly and kept my comments very neutral. I didn't want to let the new resident know my opinion of the Welcoming Committee as I might want him to take my place on it one day.

I sat at my usual table. Donna and Matthew joined me. Joan wasn't usually late. I suggested to Donna that maybe Jean was busy at work, but Donna informed me that Joan hadn't gone to work today.

"I think Joan wanted to meet the new resident who moved in today. You know she is always trying to meet a rich next husband." We all agreed that was Joan's goal.

"But," I added, "this resident seems quite old."

"All the better," Donna responded.

Time to change the subject. I asked Matthew if he knew Thomas. Matthew had lived in Port Perry for a while. Matthew's response was not what I expected. "I worked for Thomas for a short period of time helping to build the zoo."

"Wow," I said. "Did you learn about the animals as you were building the cages?"

"No," Matthew said. He left the table. I thought it was time for me to leave as well. Something had seemed to put our little group in a foul mood.

After lunch I quickly returned to my apartment to feed Ryder. She would sulk all afternoon if I didn't feed her on time. Then I realized I hadn't picked up my mail while I was downstairs. I went back to the lobby to get my mail, which was delivered every day about noon, but unfortunately I didn't pick it up every day.

Our receptionist, Tammy, looked harried. I asked her if everything was okay.

"There are two people moving in today. One is a very nice gentleman who I am sure you will get to know eventually." Apparently, she didn't know I was on the Welcoming Committee.

On my way back to my apartment, I thought I should stop at the seventh floor to make sure everything was going smoothly.

Thomas's family was getting things set up. In spite of Karen's warning not to get involved, I thought I should go in and ask if they needed help. *What the heck, no one else was there and they may have some questions.* Thomas was very polite, so I thought he would be a great addition to our bridge club. I was telling him about the various activities, including the bridge club, as his daughter was hanging up his clothes. "You have a very caring family," I said. "You are very lucky to get all this help on your move-in day." I just briefly spoke to the grandson, Timothy, before he announced that he wanted to go to the bistro for a coffee.

"Don't mind Timothy," Thomas's daughter, Corrine, said. "He will be back before we leave." Corrine was a single mother who had raised Timothy by herself while maintaining a job as a teaching assistant at a North Toronto school. She was a bit younger than I, so I asked her about her father. He seemed quite a lot older than she. Apparently, Thomas had been married twice. His son, Colin, was the product of the first marriage, and Corrine's mother was Thomas's second wife.

"That's the reason my father is leaving everything to my brother, Colin. Timothy believes it's because I was a single parent, but my father helped me financially while I was raising

Timothy. I couldn't have done it without my father's help. He was my biggest supporter."

Too much information, I thought. But she did seem like a nice, caring daughter. Maybe she thought that my having this information would help Thomas as he tried to adjust to his new surroundings.

Thomas's family was getting ready to leave as I left to go back to my apartment. I realized that Timothy had not returned. He was probably enjoying talking with some of the other residents in the bistro.

When I got to the elevator, I pushed the Up button and was glad when the car came almost immediately. Although Corrine seemed nice, I was starting to think that there was something creepy about that family. She had given me too much information about their family without any prompting or interest, from me. Mentioning what was in her father's will in front of him was thoughtless of her. And why would the grandson know what was in the will? Timothy had answered everyone, including his grandfather, in a surly tone. I hoped Thomas was going to be different from the other two.

Safely back in my apartment, I got myself ready for dinner in the dining room. There was lasagna on the menu this evening, which was one of my favourites.

When I got to the table, Joan was the one who announced, "Did you hear? The police were here this afternoon. Apparently one of the new residents who just moved in on the seventh floor was stabbed." This led to a discussion about the people who were moving into our building. I stayed out of that conversation because it was such upsetting news to me. The only person I knew who had moved in today was Thomas, and when I left his apartment, everyone there seemed to be enjoying each other's company. I couldn't believe Thomas's son or daughter would do that to their father. I didn't recall seeing Timothy after our initial introduction. The only other person who knew him was John, from the Welcoming Committee. When Karen introduced his name the other evening at the committee meeting, no one seemed to have heard of him, or at least they didn't admit it at the meeting. I didn't like the thought that one of us was a killer, but who else could it be?

Our dinner conversation was not up to our usual witty banter. I guess we were all feeling a little concerned about this news, although not concerned enough to skip the strawberry mousse for dessert. I told the others at my table that I was considering using the treadmill for my morning exercise instead of the bike. Donna mentioned that she preferred the bike and would miss our daily competition. Matthew said he preferred walking outside to using the treadmill. He suggested I join one of his walking tours. It was a great suggestion; certainly walking in the fresh air was preferable to inside. "Okay," I said. "I will continue my morning routine of using the bike."

Matthew walked each of us to our respective apartments. It was not like him to be such a gentleman, but I guessed the news had affected him more than I realized. After dropping off the other two at their apartments, he confided in me that he knew Thomas more than he had admitted at lunch. Matthew had done some carpentry work for the Port Perry Zoo, and apparently Thomas was not a nice man. Matthew said while he was working at the zoo, he didn't talk to one employee who liked working for Thomas. The employees stayed because of the animals. "He didn't treat me very well either. That was one job that I was glad when it was finished. I imagine there are a lot of people who don't like him."

As Matthew walked away, I thought, *I hope most of them were not angry enough to stab him.* It can't be easy to be a CEO of any organization. It would be difficult to please everyone.

I sat down to look at the activity calendar for the rest of the week. Tomorrow morning, I could go to the gym and then go directly to the Pilates class. I sat down to watch my game shows before starting on my homework for the writing class tomorrow afternoon.

I decided I would go to the book club this evening. They were discussing a book I had really enjoyed reading recently. Violet led the book club now that Carmen was gone. Her leadership style was similar to Carmen's. I was interested in other people's opinion of this book and was wondering if anyone had seen anything the other day.

I got to the meeting room and sat beside Caroline. She and I talked about her new daughter-in-law, Jessica. Caroline really liked Jessica and was happy that her son had found someone at last. Then Caroline told me, "I was talking with Vanessa today. You know she uses the janitor's washroom on the seventh floor because she doesn't think she can afford her water bill. This way she's not using her water when she flushes the toilet. Anyway, the other day she was very upset because there was a gentleman in that washroom for a long time. Vanessa was unable to wait and had to go back to her own apartment to use the washroom."

I was very interested in this news. "Thank you for telling me, Caroline. I wonder if there is some support for Vanessa besides using a public washroom when she can."

I imagined Vanessa's fears were unfounded. One doesn't live in downtown Toronto if one can't afford a 30-dollar water bill. There were a lot of less expensive places to live. But then, who was I to judge?

I left the meeting thinking of this interesting news.

Thomas's grandson had been gone from his apartment for a long time yesterday afternoon. I wondered if it was the same time. Thomas's apartment was just around the corner from the janitor's washroom. I would check with Daniel tomorrow morning to look at the security video. In the meantime, Violet, who left at the same time as I did, said she wanted to talk to me. We went back to the bistro. She told me that she knew some of Thomas's family, sharing that his daughter, Corrine, worked at the same school where she had worked. Violet was a teacher and Corrine, again, was a teacher's assistant.

"She was not a nice person. She was nice to the students, but she didn't like any of the teachers at the school," Violet told me. She thought for a moment, then added, "Corrine struggled financially. We could all tell she didn't have a lot of money."

I went back to my apartment thinking that Corrine seemed to be doing okay now, but maybe not. Maybe she was still struggling financially. Sometimes it was hard to determine. If she was comparing herself to her father, she wouldn't feel like she had enough money.

The next morning, I decided I needed something more than cereal for breakfast, so I scrambled up some eggs and fried some bacon. The frying bacon reminded Ryder that it was way past her breakfast time, so before I could enjoy mine, I fixed her a special breakfast. By the time I finally sat down to eat my own breakfast, I realized Donna was probably finished in the gym. I would just relax and enjoy my eggs and bacon.

While I was able to enjoy my food, I couldn't relax as I was thinking about this murder. I was starting to get an idea about what could have happened and why, but I had learned not to contact Detective Handsome until I had some hard evidence. I would ask around some more before contacting him.

At the creative writing group meeting in the bistro this

morning, I asked Malcolm if he had seen someone whom he didn't know on the seventh floor. He said that he hadn't. I thought maybe I should change the way I was asking this question. I was beginning to think that being an investigator would not be an easy job. Malcolm may have known Thomas and his family before moving into the Maple Leaf.

I left the bistro when the creative writing group meeting was finished. Walking out of the room with Louise, I asked her if she had heard anything about this incident. Malcolm was leaving at the same time. When we got out of the bistro, he yelled at me, "How can you be so insensitive? The man was stabbed and there is his grandson just over there." Timothy, who was in the living room attached to the bistro, had been waiting for our meeting to finish to buy a drink at the bar. I wondered how Malcolm knew that Thomas had been stabbed. I didn't even know that. I decided I would try to talk to Malcolm later.

I still had lots of time before dinner, so I thought I would go to the track across the road. When I got to the lobby, I saw Bob. I asked him where Doug was this afternoon. He told me that Doug was in the south garden checking on the seedlings. We both decided to go there. The south garden was beautiful. I loved that it was right on the corner of a downtown street. On the way to the horticultural room, Bob said almost in a whisper, "I will tell you a secret. We took some of the flowers from the ninth-floor terrace and moved them here." I laughed.

"Don't tell Karen," I said in an equally quiet voice. When we got to the garden, I looked around and noticed that Timothy had followed us. What a shame he hadn't joined us. He probably hadn't heard what we were saying because he was a short distance away. I told Doug and Bob that the flowers looked amazing. It was such a beautiful afternoon, I walked back to the main lobby from outside.

When I got inside, I looked for Renee.

I had planned to go to the track across the road from our building, which I liked to walk around three or four times. It was fun to watch the children trying to play soccer as I walked. I needed something to help calm me. Renee and I had previously made arrangements to do this walk together. While I was looking for Renee, I noticed Rhonda sitting in one of the chairs. She beckoned me over and told me in a loud voice that she knew that Thomas's family was refusing to pay the moving company for his recent move to this building. I wondered how she knew this information and why she thought I would be interested. I looked around for Renee and noticed Timothy looking at Rhonda and me. He didn't appear very happy. I wouldn't have either if people were discussing my family's financial business. Fortunately, at that point Renee came over, and we went across the road for our walk. It was a beautiful late afternoon, and there were several children on the field. During our walk, Renee told me she'd known Thomas's family prior to moving here. That surprised me because I thought Renee had lived in Toronto, Anyway, she told me that Thomas's family did not get along at all. They may have appeared to be caring towards Thomas, but they didn't like him at all. As we were finishing our walk, I looked behind us and saw Timothy walking around the track, not too far from us.

I thought I had it figured out, but I wanted to check out one more point before I called Detective Handsome with my theory. I went back to the Maple Leaf with Renee. She went back to her apartment, and I returned to mine.

The next morning I got up early and had a relaxing breakfast. The first person I wanted to talk was the concierge.

I went down to the lobby to get yesterday's mail. Luckily on the desk was my favourite concierge, Daniel.

I asked Daniel if the camera in the bistro was functional. He informed me that it most certainly was, so I asked to see the tape of Tuesday afternoon. "There doesn't seem to be a tape for Tuesday afternoon. You see, the camera works only when there is movement in the room, and there wasn't a function in the bistro on Tuesday afternoon. No one was in the room."

Well, that confirmed my one theory. I quickly went to the boardroom for the trivia activity. Luckily, there was an empty seat beside John. Before I got a chance to sit down, Karen came up beside me and, almost snarling, said, "I heard you interfered with Thomas's move-in. And now look what's happened. We lost a very important resident because of you." I was shocked. First, Thomas's death had nothing to do with me. Second, how had Karen found out that I was there at all? The only people I was aware who knew about my visiting apartment 745 were my three friends. I didn't think they would tell Karen.

I missed my opportunity to ask John if he knew Thomas. By the time my confrontation with Karen was finished, the trivia activity had started. I decided to talk to Vanessa, thinking I would give the seventh floor a try. She may be in the hallway. I did find Vanessa coming out of the janitor's washroom. That was a discussion for another day.

I asked Vanessa about the man in the washroom yesterday. She described him and then said, "There he is, going into that apartment." I thanked her and promised her I would meet up with her soon. On the way back to the elevator, I noted that the apartment that the gentleman whom Vanessa recognized from yesterday had gone into was number 745. I believed I now had the evidence I needed to call Detective Handsome. I quickly went back to my apartment and, ignoring Ryder's pleas for food, made the phone call.

When I told Detective Handsome what I had learned, he warned me not to do anything until he got there. After my close escape in the garbage room, I willingly agreed. He also said, "I just have to confirm one detail before I make my way over there."

Okay, I thought, *I will go downstairs to an early dinner while I wait for him. That way I can see him coming into the building through the front doors.*

I got myself ready, putting on my new skirt and a pair of new shoes, and was leaving my apartment when I remembered that I hadn't put on my lipstick. I went back into my apartment and fixed that problem. Now maybe I wouldn't have time for dinner before Handsome arrived, but I could invite him to have dinner with us after.

I got in the elevator on my floor and pushed the button for the ground floor. One floor down, a man got in. I recognized him as Thomas's grandson and tried not to look scared, but honestly, I was. He immediately started yelling at me.

"You interfering old woman. Why have you been asking so many questions of everyone?"

Old seemed a little harsh even if he was upset. There was no need for that kind of language.

I thought I would try the innocent approach. "I don't know what you mean." He immediately put his hands around my throat. I looked; we were only at the fourth floor. I had to try to fight him off, so I fought, slapping and kicking the best I could, until the door finally opened and there looking disapprovingly was Detective Handsome.

"I didn't do anything, I promise you," I said as I almost fell into his supportive arms.

DEATH IN THE DINING ROOM

This morning, I checked the schedule for the day on my computer while I was having my morning coffee. I noticed that the Pilates class was this afternoon. Twice a week we had the option of going to a Pilates class. The instructor would come here to our building so we didn't have to go to her studio. I had never taken Pilates before I moved here, but I thought I would try it when I moved in. I was glad I had made that decision. Pilates was a good way to stretch my muscles. Plus, I'd met some really nice people through this class, including the instructor.

After lunch, I dressed in my sweatpants and sweatshirt and went to the Pilates class. There were only a few of us who attended. In my opinion, that was a bonus. It allowed the instructor to concentrate on teaching us the proper way to do the moves. I had really been enjoying this class. I stood beside Phyllis, who was much better at Pilates than I. She was a tall, thin woman who looked much too young to be in this building, but I appreciated her being here. She and I talked on a regular basis. We didn't usually have our meals at the same time as each other, but I saw her in some of the other activities we each attended. Today Phyllis was wearing tights and an athletic T-shirt. She looked as if she knew what she was doing.

Roberta was also wearing tights and an athletic T-shirt. I started to feel shabby in my sweatpants and sweatshirt.

During the class, Graham joined us. It wasn't like him to be late; he was usually very punctual. He stood beside me, looking uncharacteristically disheveled. I was grateful that he had stood beside me. That is, until he started talking through the instructor's instructions. I realized he was in quite a foul mood, and his language matched his mood. At one point, he started doing tai chi moves. Either that or he was stabbing an imaginary foe. I decided to turn my attention to Phyllis. She was much more pleasant and she was listening to the instructor, which allowed me to listen.

I didn't think the class was over, as we hadn't completed our stretches, but Graham stormed out. I heard him say something about the waitresses as he left.

The class today was more intense than usual. I definitely hadn't needed the sweatshirt. That was okay because I saw the menu for tonight's dinner posted in the lobby. I needed to burn off extra calories if I wanted to enjoy dinner without feeling guilty.

The Pilates class finished midafternoon, which gave me plenty of time to get showered and dressed for dinner. I met my usual friends, Donna, Joan and Matthew, at our usual table.

Donna was still wearing her exercise clothes. I asked her about that. She said that after dinner, she was planning to go jogging around the track across the street from the Maple Leaf. What an excellent idea. I usually just walked briskly, but I could give jogging a try. I thought I would join her. Donna didn't need to lose weight, but the jogging helped to keep her limber—and actually it helped to keep our minds clear. I told her I would quickly change after dinner and join her. Matthew, who didn't need to lose any weight either, said he would not be able to join us as he was meeting some friends this evening to go to a local pub.

Joan thought the jogging was a great idea and said she would join us. Joan didn't usually go to the exercise classes during the day. I wasn't sure if she walked or jogged usually, but she did go around the track on a regular basis. Some of the people in our building regularly walked or strolled around the ninth-floor terrace. That was another good option we would have to try one evening. As well as getting some exercise, we would get to enjoy the beautiful flowers that Elaine and her committee had planted.

Joan started to talk about her day at Smith's Shoes. Just as she was telling us about her two co-workers who didn't get along, we heard yelling coming from the kitchen. I excused myself to go there to see if I could help. When I got to just outside the kitchen, I heard, "How dare you show up here? Why don't you leave?" I didn't recognize the voices, and seeing as it was a personal fight, I thought I should go back to my table. I got back to my seat in time to hear the end of the shoe discussion. As I'd always suspected, the salespeople where Joan worked were on commission. There was one particularly aggressive salesperson who seemed to know which customers would be quick and easy sales, so she would make sure she got to them first. I guess all workplaces are the same.

The argument in the kitchen got so loud that the kitchen manager, Michelle, was called in to intervene. She didn't look too happy as she went into the kitchen. I didn't blame her. Things usually ran very smoothly in the dining room, and this didn't sound too professional. The background noise I liked to hear during a meal was some easy listening dinner music. Michelle came back out of the kitchen very quickly and advised everyone to stay in their seats. Soon, the police arrived. This was obviously more than just an argument.

Detective Hanson, or Detective Handsome as I thought of him, and his team started to interview everyone in the dining room. They started with the tables closest to the kitchen. We had a long wait before Detective Handsome himself came to our table. In the meantime, our group had started talking with the people at the table beside ours: Phyllis, Janet, Bob and Doug.

It was finally our turn to be interviewed. As Detective Handsome turned towards our table, one of his people began interviewing Phyllis's table. Handsome's interview didn't take too long. He asked us if we had heard anything. We all explained about the commotion we had heard coming from the kitchen at the beginning of dinner.

Detective Handsome told our table, "The new waitress has been killed. I don't think it is anything any of you need to be concerned about. My team will do a thorough job of investigating this crime."

Was he looking directly at me as he said that? I thought so.

Then he asked if any of us had heard any rumours about the kitchen staff. We all said we hadn't heard anything.

This time he definitely turned to me. He asked, "Are you sure?"

I replied indignantly, saying that I was sure. Really, did he think I was nosey? I didn't think I was. I was a little annoyed. Sometimes Detective Handsome could be very insensitive.

I was still a little miffed about this later that evening while I was enjoying my evening treat. I was almost finished when there was a knock at the door. It was Handsome. I let him in and offered him some tea. He said he couldn't stay because they were still working downstairs in the kitchen.

He told me, "I just wanted to apologize if I offended you during the interview earlier. You sounded annoyed when you answered. I would never knowingly offend you."

Now I felt bad for having been annoyed. He sounded quite apologetic. With fingers crossed behind my back, I told him, "No, I wasn't offended."

As he left, he said, "Please try not to get involved in this one. It looks nasty." I promised him I would try to stay out of it. This time I didn't have my fingers crossed.

Once Handsome had left, I told Ryder, "I will try to stay out of this case." While I don't think cats can roll their eyes, I think Ryder tried to roll hers.

Feeling mollified by Handsome's apology, I went back to my tea and treat, but it was difficult to enjoy with a disapproving cat sitting on the arm of my chair. For such a large cat, she was able to balance herself on thin surfaces.

The next morning on my way to the lobby, I met Janet in the elevator. She told me that one of the new residents, Lucy, knew the waitress who had been killed, from another facility. The waitress was apparently good at her job and hadn't caused any problems there. While Janet was talking, I wondered how Lucy knew it was a waitress who had been killed and how she knew which one it was.

I asked Janet if Lucy had told her who it was who had gotten killed. I didn't remember Detective Handsome telling us her name in our interview.

Janet got flustered and couldn't remember who had told her that it was the new waitress who'd been killed. I was amazed at how fast gossip or rumours spread, especially when it was bad news. I felt bad about flustering Janet because it was always such a pleasure to talk with her. I didn't think Janet was trying to spread gossip. Conversation with Janet was always very positive. Maybe it was because she was quite new to the building, but she always found positive things to say about people and the building.

Janet was taller than I. Still, I was only five feet three inches, so most people were taller than I am. She had short white hair and was always smiling. I wished her a good day and went to the front desk to drop off the package that I was putting in the mail.

One of my friends had just become a grandmother, so in my knitting class, I had knitted a blanket for the new little boy. I had chosen light green because I knew it would take me awhile to complete it, and when I first started it, I didn't know if the baby was going to be a girl or a boy. I finished my business with the front desk and was headed for the elevator when I saw Malcolm sitting in the lobby looking out the front window.

I went over to say hello to him. What a difference from talking to Janet. Malcolm was usually very cranky, but today he surprised me. He told me, "I heard that one of the waitresses has been killed. I don't know which one it was, but I'm sorry to hear this news because I really like all the waitresses. In fact, one of them always brought me extra dessert."

I asked him, "Did you know her name?"

He replied in a pleasant tone, "No, I never got her name, but she was fairly new."

I wished him a good day and went to pick up my mail while I was downstairs.

The mail was delivered to our mailboxes in early afternoon. With the Pilates class yesterday afternoon, I hadn't gotten my mail. I figured the bills and flyers could wait one more day. I was correct. My mail consisted of just bills and flyers.

Relieved of my big package and armed with this week's

flyers, I headed up to the twelfth floor. When I got there, I noticed a few people gathered outside Matthew's apartment. I heard some laughing, so I decided everything must be okay. I went to check out what was going on.

I heard Matthew telling the group that he had heard from Stan that the chef was having an affair with the waitress. They knew each other from a previous residence. I wasn't sure that was a good reason to murder someone, but I left them to their gossiping. I had a hungry cat to deal with.

When I got inside my apartment, the phone was ringing. It was Jaime calling to ask if I wanted to meet at the Creamery King for lunch. "Of course," I said, agreeing quickly. "I can be there in fifteen minutes." Jaime sounded relieved, so I was glad I was available.

On my way out the front door, I was stopped by Larry. He wanted to tell me that Renee regularly sat at his table. I felt bad for Larry, but I wasn't sure why he was telling me this. Then he explained. Renee was sure she had seen Louise going into the kitchen just before the yelling started.

I asked Larry if that was even possible. I wasn't sure that Renee had a view of the kitchen door from where she usually sat.

Larry assured me that Renee not only had a view of the door, but also watched that door carefully every meal after placing her order. She complained to the rest of the table when the waitresses came out the door with plates and didn't bring a plate to her.

Although his mealtimes sounded stressful, I wasn't sure why he was telling me this. I thanked him for the information and wished him a great day.

I quickly left the building and started walking in the direction of the local Creamery King.

When I got to the CK, I saw Jaime sitting at an outside

table. She had buttons with her. I had forgotten about Buttons when I agreed to this lunch. The darn dog nipped at my ankles. For a small dog with such a cute name, he really was very miserable. Oh well, I would enjoy lunch and the conversation. I lifted my feet off the ground, trying to avoid the dog. Jaime, who had just recently moved in, was enjoying the Maple Leaf and thought it was the best move she had ever made. I agreed. There were a lot of activities, and we both agreed that we really liked the community feeling we all had.

Then Jaime told me that she had heard that the chef was having an affair with one of the residents. She wasn't sure which one it was because she had heard two names—Louise and Roberta. I was surprised our chef had time to make our dinners. This possible new information might change my idea of the importance of Larry's comment. Now I wished I had asked him more information. I would have to try to find him later, maybe at the art class later this afternoon.

I tried to change the subject, but of course this murder was on everyone's mind right now. I asked if Jaime liked the food at the Maple Leaf. She said she really enjoyed it. I agreed with her; it was delicious. It might just have been because I wasn't the one who had to cook it and do the dishes afterwards, but I really appreciated the dinners in the dining room.

Then Jaime told me that Anjelica and Graham were not happy with the food. They were apparently especially unhappy with the servers. Jaime told me they often complained to her that their food is cold when it gets to their table. Jaime agreed with me that she had never had that problem. Maybe once when my tablemates and I got into a heated debate and let our food sit there while we finished our discussion it was cool. But it always arrived at our table hot or at least warm.

We finished our lunch and started to walk back to the

Maple Leaf in time for our art class activity. On the walk back, Phyllis joined us. That was pleasant. I thought she would give Buttons more ankles to nip at and he might leave mine alone. No such luck. I wasn't sure what it was, but he liked my ankles. Maybe I would try a different soap. Lewis may have an idea which soap would repel dogs. I would have to ask him when we got back.

On our walk, we were enjoying looking at the old houses in this section of the city. I really enjoyed the architecture from that era. I would ask Matthew about it, but it may be easier to just go on one of his tours.

Phyllis interrupted my reverie, saying, "Did either of you hear that Alice and Stan are splitting up? Alice thinks that Stan has been too friendly with the new waitress, and she's sick of his constant flirting with her." I let Phyllis know that the new waitress was gone.

Jaime asked us, "Would that be a motive for murder?" She added, "If that was the motive, wouldn't it be Stan that Alice killed?"

I was not enjoying this macabre conversation at all. Fortunately, we were close to the Maple Leaf. I changed the subject by asking the two of them if they could hear the children playing in the schoolyard.

Just then, one of the children screeched. I was very glad my apartment was on the twelfth floor.

When we finally reached our building, Jaime stayed outside to give Buttons one last walk before taking him up to her apartment. Phyllis wanted to take her groceries up to her unit.

We all wished each other a great day as we went our separate ways. On my way to art class, I met up with William. He informed me that he had heard Janet and Matthew were a couple.

I didn't think this information was true, and I told him so. I wished people would verify their facts before spreading gossip.

I met up with Phyllis in the library on the ninth floor of our building after art class. I had gone there to find a book by my favourite local author. Phyllis was using the computer. I was trying not to disturb her, but she came over to me, seeming very worried. She told me that a few of the people at her table told the police that they had heard a voice yelling in the kitchen last night that they didn't recognize. "Can anyone just walk into our building through the kitchen?" she asked me.

It was an excellent question, one I didn't have an answer for. We talked for a while longer but still couldn't answer her question. More importantly, we couldn't answer why anyone would want to come in and kill the waitress. Phyllis didn't have any gossip to share about the kitchen staff. I appreciated that. I had been learning too much about the kitchen staff lately.

She did tell me that she had joined the Welcoming Committee. Apparently, Karen tricked her into joining. I was pleased that some more nice people were joining the committee.

I had to admit, dinner was a little eerie this evening. The food was delicious, but it was just unsettling to be in the dining room. It didn't help that none of my friends were there.

I finished eating quite quickly and then headed back to my apartment. Before I got back, I thought I should check out the kitchen door myself. It wasn't that late. There were still some people eating their dinner. I went past Donna's apartment and asked her if she would join me in checking out if the kitchen door was locked.

"Yes, let's do it!" she exclaimed.

Neither of us had tried to get into the kitchen from the outside before, so it could take awhile to find the correct door. We both agreed that it probably wasn't marked. We went out the front door and then went to the side of our building where the kitchen would be. On the way, I told Donna about Phyllis's concern.

Donna agreed with Phyllis: The door should be locked. Then we both stopped dead in our tracks. Donna looked at me as she realized what that meant.

"If the door is locked, that means someone from the Maple Leaf did it! That means someone in the kitchen or a resident stabbed the waitress," she said. I was thinking the same thing.

Then we both agreed that it would be eerie to go back into the dining room to eat. I knew this for a fact. Donna would find out tomorrow at lunch.

We got to the door that we both had decided was probably the kitchen door. I tried it. It was locked.

Donna said, "Before we jump to any disturbing conclusions, let me go back inside and through the kitchen. I will open the door from the inside. That will confirm if this is the kitchen door."

It was a great idea. Although I wasn't sure who I was more afraid for. If the murderer was one of the kitchen staff, I wasn't sure Donna would be safe in the kitchen. On the other hand, this door opened onto a really scary-looking alley. As I was waiting, my imagination was going wild. I jumped at every sound I heard, unsure if an animal or a person would have been more terrifying. Probably an animal. Luckily, I didn't have to wait too long. After about fifteen minutes, Donna opened the door. She quickly came out the door and closed it. Then she said, "I don't mind telling you. That was scary."

On the walk back to the main door, we both talked about the fact that it would be really unnerving to eat in the dining room until this murder was solved. We walked back to our apartments together. I walked Donna to her door because she was probably more alarmed than I was, if that was possible.

When I got back to my apartment, I made myself a pot of tea and started to think about what Donna and I had just learned. If someone had come in the door, they would have to have had a key or would have to have been expected. It still pointed to a staff member committing the murder. Then I started to think about the details I had learned over the last few days. I seemed to be getting all sorts of dirt about people and a lot of suspects and motives, but I wasn't any farther along to solving the crime. I was beginning to appreciate just how difficult Detective Handsome's job was. Deciding to take the evening off and drink my tea, I put my feet up and watched my game shows.

The next morning while making my morning coffee, I decided to try a different angle for determining who murdered the waitress, so I decided to talk to my favourite concierge, Daniel. Before I bothered him with my request, I thought I should phone Donna. I had told her that yesterday I hadn't seen a security camera at the door. "Oh, I saw one on the inside. I should have mentioned it yesterday, but I just wanted to get out of there," she said.

That made sense. The pictures from a camera on the outside of the door could be affected by weather or darkness, or get stolen. I went downstairs to see if Donald was available. He was at the front desk, so I asked him if I could see the security tape for the evening of the murder.

When I told him what I was looking for, he said, "It's not very helpful. No one came in the kitchen door except Michael's wife. She goes into the kitchen quite often while he is working."

I thanked him for his help and wished him a good day. While I was downstairs, I figured I might as well walk over to the Maple Leaf Espresso and get a latte. On my way out the door, Donna stopped me. "Did you hear that the new waitress was pregnant when she was murdered?" she asked.

"No. I had no idea." I didn't hear the rest of what Donna was saying. *This changes everything*, I thought. I went back to my apartment to think about what this meant. Then I phoned Detective Handsome to tell him what I had found out.

I also told him my theory.

"I will be right over. Please stay in your apartment until I get there." He wanted to confront the murderer. I thought I would take his advice. As I waited for him, I combed my hair and changed my clothes.

When Handsome arrived, he pulled out his hand-held computer and looked a few things up. "I will be back in two hours. Please stay here until I return, and then I will explain everything," he said. He scratched Ryder's ear then quickly left, going out the door. I hadn't had a chance to go get my latte or read the paper this morning, so I made myself a cup of coffee and read the paper while I waited for Handsome to return, which he did exactly two hours later.

He explained that they had arrested Michael's wife. The waitress, Carla, was not pregnant. The other waitresses didn't like her because in previous retirement homes she had managed to get all the good shifts. She was upset, and when Michael's wife came through the kitchen door, she saw that Michael had his arm around Carla, trying to console her because she had been crying. Michael's wife misunderstood this innocent gesture and assumed Carla was having an affair with him.

"Michael swore to us and to his wife that he was not having an affair with Carla.

"Good detective work, Sara. And I'm glad you stayed safe this time," Detective Handsome said. I just beamed.

MURDER OF A FRIEND

When I woke up this morning, it looked like such a beautiful sunny day that I thought I would go for a walk around the track that was across the road instead of using the bike in the gym. I texted Donna to ask if she would join me, but she preferred the bike, so I was on my own.

By the time I got Ryder her breakfast, it wasn't too early. I thought maybe I could meet someone in the lobby who wanted to join me.

In the elevator on the way down to the lobby, I was trying to determine why some people sat in the lobby for hours at a time. I supposed it was so they could see other people. When I got to the lobby, there were a few people sitting there. I asked one of the men, Harold, who wasn't reading a paper, if he wanted to go for a walk with me. He accepted immediately. I thought he might. According to Thelma, Harold hadn't made many friends since he moved in.

We got to the track and started walking. Harold was a fast walker. I had trouble keeping up with him, but I managed, although I was panting as I was trying to talk with him. Was he trying to get away from me? Or was he annoyed? This was going to be a good workout. I asked him if he enjoyed it here at the Maple Leaf. He told me gruffly that he was enjoying the activities and most of the people. He started to sound angry when he told me that there was one person who really aggravated him.

I changed the subject. If he was going to start complaining about some of the people here, I didn't want to hear it. I had my own list of people I could complain about, but I kept my griping to myself.

I asked him about his home. A number of the new residents had an issue with getting used to living in an apartment after having lived in large houses their whole lives. Now I knew for sure that he was very angry with me because he was yelling at me as he informed me that he had managed to sell his multimillion-dollar home before he moved in. Okay, it didn't answer my question, but it was obviously an off-limits topic as well.

We walked silently while I was trying to come up with a neutral topic that wouldn't anger him. We were back on the side of the track that was closest to the Maple Leaf. Alice and Stan crossed the road and came on to the track. They were a very nice older couple who seemed very social. They both attended a lot of activities here at the Maple Leaf. I quickly introduced them to Harold and headed back to the main lobby.

It was still a beautiful day. I went up to the ninth-floor terrace. On the way there I tried not to feel guilty for what I had done to Alice and Stan. I consoled myself with the thought that maybe they had been able to come up with a topic of conversation that didn't anger Harold. I had talked with Harold before and thought he was a nice man. Maybe he was just having a bad morning.

I got to the terrace. William, a well-dressed older gentleman with thick glasses, was there. I was glad for the company.

I sat beside William on one of the benches. He told me that

he had known both Harold and Howard before moving to the Maple Leaf. He said, "Harold and Howard seemed to get along before, or at least tolerated each other. I never realized there was a feud between them. Something has happened recently to start it or intensify it. Even here at the Maple Leaf, they were never as angry with each other as I have observed lately. Yes, they maybe complained about each other, but who of us doesn't complain?"

We both came up with some suggestions for what might have intensified the feud, but neither of us could come up with a rational reason for why this feud had escalated recently.

As William was talking, I was admiring his glasses. I thought I needed a new pair soon, so I asked him where he had gotten his. This started a long conversation about the importance of eye exams. He told me where he got his eyes checked and where he got his glasses. I would have to look into this further.

As I was getting on the elevator to go up to the twelfth floor, I was stopped by Clara. She was a nice older woman, so I didn't mind stopping to talk to her. "I have some important information to tell you," she said, looking proud of herself. Then she blurted out, "I know who stole the money!"

I just thought to myself, *This is a mystery for another day. I don't want to start investigating this crime now.*

Then I thought this might be a good case for Detective Handsome. If he was able to solve the case of the missing money, it may help his career. So I asked her who she thought did it.

She told me, "It had to be the president of the company. He was the only one who really knew the finances of the company, and he knew that the company could survive losing that much money. If the company closed down, the theft would have been investigated earlier." I asked her how she knew this. She told me that her husband used to work on the line at Scarborough Mechanical Belts. Everyone on the line talked about it at the time. It was the reason they hadn't gotten a wage increase that year.

"Who was the president?" I asked Clara. Unfortunately, she didn't remember. But then, it would be easy enough to find out on the Internet.

Just then Clara's daughter came into the lobby to take her mother to her doctor's appointment. "Don't tell my daughter I told you this," she whispered to me as her daughter came over.

I headed back to the elevator to go to my apartment. On the way up, I debated with myself if I should tell Detective Handsome this information. I thought the evidence Clara had provided was pretty weak. On the other hand, it would be good for the police to solve this. On a purely selfish level, I thought that then I wouldn't have to hear about it anymore. I made up my mind: I would contact Detective Handsome tomorrow morning. That would give me time to try to find some more information about the people involved. I just relaxed the rest of the morning, knowing the afternoon would be busy.

I did get myself dressed properly for lunch in the dining room. They were going to be serving Cobb salad, so I made sure to get to the dining room in time. I met my friends at our usual table.

Joan said everyone at work this morning had gotten along. Wow. That didn't usually happen.

Matthew told us about a new tour he was creating. It sounded amazing. They would walk around the neighbourhood looking for plants that would attract bumblebees. My day was definitely getting better.

I was very glad to see that we were all in such good moods.

I didn't want to spoil the atmosphere by telling my friends about my morning walk, but I did tell everyone about my cinnamon bun. Matthew thought maybe he would create a tour of cafes and bakeries in the neighbourhood. I would definitely go on that tour.

After my salad, I didn't need dessert because of the cinnamon bun I had just finished eating shortly before lunch. So I left the table before the others, wishing them a great afternoon. I knew my afternoon would be great.

Before I was able to go back to my apartment and start one of my favourite tasks, there was the art class activity I wanted to attend. I could not draw at all, but in this activity, the instructor gave us a step-by-step method for drawing, or sometimes we used paints. One of the creations was beautiful. Mine usually looked a little bit like what it was supposed to be, but nowhere near as polished as the others. But I enjoyed myself and got an opportunity to talk to someone other than just Ryder.

Sitting beside me today was Ray. He told me that Leonard must have committed the robbery at Scarborough Mechanical Belts and framed the other two. He told me he had come to that conclusion because Harold and Howard were not good at their jobs. Harold had been put in his position of CFO because his uncle was the president of Scarborough Mechanical Belts. Harold thought Howard knew what he was doing and kept promoting him. Leonard was the only person in the department who knew anything about accounting. He had his CA designation. The other two had no designations. When I looked confused, he explained about the different designations that accountants could get. Actually, I enjoyed my conversation with Ray. I looked over at the butterfly that he'd drawn. It looked like a real butterfly. Mine looked pretty good as well. Maybe step-by-step was a good way for me to create artwork.

The class was over, so everyone, including me, left the room. I thought I might as well get my mail while I waited for the elevator. The elevator would be busy. After I picked up my mail, I sat in one of the comfortable chairs by the window, enjoying the sunshine for just a few minutes. Ray came and sat beside me.

This was perfect because I wanted to follow up on what he had told me in our class. It was intriguing. I asked him, "Are you sure about the robbery? Even if a person was bad at his job, that's a lot of money to lose."

Ray chuckled and told me, "You are correct. Howard must have stolen the money from Scarborough Mechanical Belts all those years ago because he lived in a very expensive house. It was beyond the price range that a controller should have been able to afford. Scarborough Mechanical Belts was not a large company, and they didn't pay their employees well."

Janice joined the conversation. "Howard's grandfather passed away just before he bought the house," she pointed out.

"No," Ray replied. "That happened after he bought the house."

I left them to continue their argument. Having nothing to add to the conversation, I thought it would be better if I just talked with Graham. He started complaining about the fact that he had to do his own laundry. Who did he think was going to do his laundry, the laundry fairy? I couldn't relate to his point of view because I had always done my own laundry. I was just thrilled to be able to do it in my own apartment. Oh well, at least he wasn't talking about a robbery that took place many years ago.

When I got back to my apartment, I changed into my grubby clothes in preparation for cleaning out the fish tank. I was in the middle of this fun, easy task. The only hitch was making sure the cat didn't get the fish while they were in their temporary home as I cleaned their main home. I had that situation under control, so I was enjoying this task.

There was a knock at my door. When I answered it, Roberta was standing there. I invited her into my apartment and asked her if she minded if I continued my task while we talked.

She answered, "No, of course not. I like fish. They are so relaxing to watch."

I agreed with her.

Then she proceeded to tell me that she had been talking with a resident who recently moved in. The resident was Leonard. She told me that he used to work with Howard and Harold. She had known Leonard when they worked at Toronto Piano Factory. She then told me that Leonard had been fired from the Scarborough Mechanical Belts factory and started working at Toronto Piano Factory.

Roberta worked in the marketing department, but it was a small office and she knew most of the people there. Leonard was a very nice person and was very good at his job. There were rumours about the theft at Scarborough Mechanical Belts. Roberta believed that Leonard knew who actually took the money. He never said who it was, but the rumour in her office was that he would know exactly what happened.

I asked Roberta, "Did Leonard know if Howard and Harold were living here before he moved in?"

Roberta replied, "I don't know for sure. I didn't ask him." She added, "He couldn't have known. I don't think he is safe here with the two of them here."

She had a good point. Although, if Leonard didn't talk about it, maybe they wouldn't realize who he was. It would also help if people like Roberta didn't talk about the situation.

The next morning, I got to the gym before Donna. I sat on

her usual bike and waited for her to show up. I didn't have to wait long. We did our usual race. Donna still beat me. Maybe it was not the bike. Maybe I had to admit that Donna was fitter than I was.

While I was riding the bike, I noticed that Howard was using the treadmill. I asked him about his job before he retired.

He told me that he had worked at Scarborough Mechanical Belts. He told me that he had served as the financial controller there. It was a great job. He started his career there and worked his way up. Matthew had mentioned this to me once before.

It did sound like a great job. But Howard never looked happy. Before I had a chance to ask him if he missed working, he told me that someone had stolen a lot of money from Scarborough Mechanical Belts while he was working there and changed the books so that it looked as if he had stolen the money. He started to sound very angry about this situation, so I thought I would try to change the subject.

I asked him if he had lived in Scarborough. I had lived in Scarborough for a long time, so I was interested to know where he lived. He told me that he had bought a house in Don Mills. That would have been an impressive piece of property, so I tried to ask him about that. He angrily changed the subject back to the alleged theft at work. By that time, my thirty minutes on the bike was finished.

After the angry conversation with Howard, I didn't mind listening to Donna's gloating over winning our race. At least it was a positive topic.

I had a full day of activities planned. Not everyone liked to go to all of the activities, which was why we had such a variety at Maple Leaf. I personally liked to keep busy, so I tried to go to most of the events. It also allowed me to keep in touch with everyone and find out what they were doing. I consider myself a very social person.

A good place I have found to get information was at the trivia activity. So after the gym I went back to my apartment to change clothes and get ready to head back to the ninth floor.

I returned to my apartment quickly and started getting myself ready for the trivia event. I was the scorekeeper, so I couldn't be late.

Just as I was about to go out the door, Donna phoned me to remind me about this event. Sometimes she could be very annoying. What, did she think I would forget to show up? Trivia was something I was very interested in. Also, a lot of people showed up to this one, so it was a good opportunity to get the latest gossip. I think she phoned to make sure I was coming because her team usually won. She liked to remind me of that at every opportunity. I got over my anger and got myself to the bistro before the activity started.

This morning, Harold and Howard both showed up to the trivia game. They didn't usually both attend the same events. According to Matthew, a very good source of gossip, they both used to work at the same company, but something happened and they don't get along at all now. Maybe I had found out what it was this morning. So my conversation wasn't a total waste. Plus, it would give me something to think about while riding the bike later.

Harold had been at the Maple Leaf as long as I had. Howard moved in a few months prior. He probably hadn't known Harold lived here when he chose this building. I wondered what really happened all those years ago. I would have to check into this further. They were both very nice gentlemen. It was a shame they didn't get along.

The trivia game ended. My team lost, but we had fun trying to answer the questions.

As we were leaving the bistro, I managed to pull Harold aside to talk to him. He had played on my team, so I asked him if he enjoyed himself and if he wanted to be on our team for future games. Harold had gotten a lot of the geography questions correct. Geography was not my specialty, so I appreciated the help for our team. I asked him if he was okay with John answering the economics or math questions. I didn't want to offend a potential asset to our team. He told me he was okay with it. "Actually, I don't really like math, and I'm not good with numbers," Harold told me. This left me speechless. I thought he had worked in the finance department at his company. Before I managed to get over my shock and ask him about this, he had left.

I decided to eat lunch in my apartment today. Without much time between the trivia game and the matinee this afternoon, I decided to make myself a cheese sandwich. The food was definitely better in the dining room, but I had to do a load of laundry and sweep the floor in my living room. Not exciting stuff, but I liked a clean, tidy apartment, so I enjoyed doing these chores. It was also a good way to avoid listening to the complaints and criticisms our table seemed to be making lately. Even Matthew seemed to be taking a side in the Howard/Harold feud.

After my cheese sandwich, I thought I deserved two cookies with my tea. Ryder gave me a disapproving look, but I continued eating. When I finished my cookies, I headed to the theatre on the ninth floor for the matinee.

On my way to the matinee, I met Leonard in the elevator. He was dressed as he usually was, in dress pants with a shirt and tie. He'd been in this building for only a short time, but he already had a reputation for being a good dresser. He also had a reputation for being a really nice guy. Every time I saw him, he had a smile and would stop and chat. Definitely not like most of the financial analysts I had known throughout my career.

I asked Leonard, "Did you know Harold or Howard before you moved into this building? They seem like interesting people."

Leonard told me that he had not known Harold and Howard were living in this building before he moved in. Then he said, "I knew them from years ago when I worked for them. I didn't enjoy working with them. I have heard the rumours, and I don't believe either of them stole the money. Neither of them knows enough accounting to be able to cover it up if they did take it." Then Leonard told me he thought they both had volatile tempers and he was actually afraid of them. He added, "They both threatened to fire me a few times if I didn't create the transactions they wanted created. They can't fire me now, of course, but I still don't like being around them."

We arrived at the ninth floor, where I got out. I quickly asked Leonard if he was coming to the movie. He just laughed and said no. Then he added, "Enjoy!"

They were playing what I considered a classic movie from the 1970s. Not everyone agreed with me, but they were entitled to their opinion. I couldn't sing, but I did enjoy all musicals. In the privacy of my own apartment, I would be singing along to this movie, but I decided to spare everyone in the theatre from having to listen to me singing off-key.

Before the matinee started, I sat down beside Phyllis. She said that she had seen me in the gym this morning talking to Howard. "After I saw Howard in the lobby yesterday, I remembered his face from a newspaper article years ago. I looked on the computer and found some of the details. His name was associated with a big robbery. The robbery was really big news when it happened," Phyllis said. Before she had a chance to tell me her theory, Janet sat beside us and had something to add to the conversation. She and Phyllis got into a debate over who stole the money. I thought we should just forget about the whole issue. It happened many years ago, but it still seemed to be causing problems, mainly for Howard and Harold. Now, however, it was causing a rift between Phyllis and Janet.

Luckily, the movie started before the discussion got too heated. It was a fun musical, so the three of us sang along. Phyllis was a very good singer. I would have to ask her to join our singalong activity. We needed more good singers. At the end of the movie, neither of them complained about my singing. Maybe I didn't give them a chance. As soon as the movie was over, I left quickly before any more discussion about this robbery started up. Janet must have had the same idea.

On my way to my apartment to get ready for dinner, I met Janet in the elevator. Wanting to avoid the previous topic, I asked her about her day. She told me that this morning she had helped a new resident get oriented. I remembered now: Janet had been picked to welcome Leonard.

Janet told me Leonard seemed like a very nice person. Then she said, "I asked him where he used to work. He worked at the Scarborough Mechanical Belts plant as a financial analyst. I used to work there as well. I didn't realize that Howard and Harold used to work there or else I would have been more interested in what Leonard was telling me."

I wondered if Leonard would eventually get along with Howard and Harold. He seemed like the type to try to get along with everyone. If he wasn't involved in their feud, he might think it a benefit to know someone in the building.

Although they both seemed angry most of the time, I was never afraid of them. Of course, I hadn't worked for them. I could see how they would be frightening bosses. *I will have to check out this intriguing trio,* I thought, as I walked down the hallway to my apartment.

Just before I got to my door, I met Matthew in the hallway. He was coming back from playing pool in the games room. He told me that Howard was very angry that Harold had moved into this building. Howard was hoping to finally get away from this scandal. I agreed with Howard. I told Matthew that I wished we would all forget about it. Then I went inside my apartment.

I texted my friend Jaime to ask if she wanted to go to Creamery King. I was even willing to tolerate Buttons just for a chance to talk with someone who would not talk about long-ago robberies. She texted me back saying that she was at the Maple Leaf Espresso sitting inside with Leonard. *Oh,* I thought. *This should be interesting.* I agreed to meet her. By the time I got there, she was sitting outside by herself. She told me that she had put Buttons in a tote bag she had for him. She had done this while she was inside talking to Leonard. "I will tell you about that conversation in a moment. But first, I have to take Buttons out of the tote bag. I will warn you; he doesn't like being in the tote bag, so he may be a little cranky," she said. He went straight for my ankles as soon as he was released. Tropical fish were so much easier to deal with.

Jaime told me that Leonard had asked her to go for a coffee so he could explain to someone why Harold and Howard didn't like each other. *Oh no, I have to listen to this story again and put up with Buttons.* But Leonard's story was different. He confessed to Jaime that the reason Harold and Howard were angry at each other was because Leonard's moving in reminded them of this incident many years ago. Leonard worked in the same finance department as the other two gentlemen. This theory made no sense to me because the other two had not been friends for years. Although perhaps Leonard's move-in had intensified their anger. Then I thought, *Don't get involved, Sara.* I changed the subject to pets and how calming it was to watch tropical fish swim around a tank with plants and pretty ornaments. Jaime didn't seem convinced, so I asked her about her opinion of Leonard.

She replied, "I really enjoyed our conversation. And I was hoping Leonard and I could get together again."

I reminded her about the bistro on the ninth floor. For bad weather days, that was a good option. We were both smiling as we walked back to the Maple Leaf.

As I was getting ready for dinner, I was discussing my interesting afternoon with Ryder. She showed her usual lack of interest, but I was grateful to have someone with whom I could talk about this. It helped. I may have detected a slight bit of compassion from her when I told her my team had lost at trivia again this morning. It was either that or the fact that I was opening her canned food at that time. That and not my story may have been what got her attention.

Going downstairs to go into the dining room, I noticed someone I didn't recognize talking to Howard in the lobby. That was interesting. I tried to get a little closer without being too noticeable so I could listen in on the conversation and try to determine who it was. Unfortunately, Clara stepped between us, so I wasn't able to hear the conversation. I did notice, however, that they both seemed to be smiling and getting along. I would have to follow up on this. Maybe Matthew would have some information. I headed into the dining room. My friends Matthew, Donna and Joan were at our usual table, so I sat down and ordered dinner: a deluxe cheeseburger. I didn't get a chance to ask Matthew about Leonard and Howard's friendship. There was already an interesting conversation going on at our table. Matthew was talking about the walking tour he had led this morning. They'd gone to Underpass Park, which I thought was such a creative use of space. I had never been there because it was too far for me to walk, but I enjoyed hearing about it from Matthew.

Joan usually attended the knitting club with me on Tuesday afternoons, so she talked about the knitting project that she was working on. The conversations seemed very positive. Maybe we were all finished with the anger being spread by Howard and Harold, or maybe we finally had found a way to deal with it.

Donna asked me if I wanted to go to Creamery King for dessert this evening. When I said I did want to go, she invited the others at our table, then announced, "It is customary for the trivia loser to pay, so Sara is buying an ice cream sundae for each of us."

Thinking, *I have got to find new friends*, I looked around the room. Howard and Harold were each sitting at a separate table by themselves. So Leonard didn't join either of them. Interesting. I wasn't sure which one was Leonard, so I wasn't sure if he had found a friend to eat with.

Janet came over to our table, and I asked her to point out Leonard. He was sitting at a table by himself on the opposite side of the dining room from Harold and Howard. I couldn't blame him.

After our delicious dinner, the four of us, Matthew, Joan, Donna and I, walked over to the Creamery King. As Donna had promised them, I paid for a treat for each of us. It was a beautiful evening to sit outside and enjoy our ice cream sundaes, the perfect ending to our dinner. We enjoyed the scenery as we walked back to the Maple Leaf. I asked the others if anyone knew Howard or Harold.

Matthew said he knew Harold from their discussions while playing pool in our games room. Matthew had never met Harold before he moved to the Maple Leaf. He had never talked with Howard but had heard stories about him from Harold.

I would definitely have to get more details from him later. Right now, I was tired of hearing about this decades-old feud that was now causing dissention in our building.

When we came in the front door, we all heard yelling coming from the dining room. I peeked in the window and saw Harold and Howard in the corner looking and sounding very angry. I couldn't make out everything that they were saying, and I didn't know their voices well enough to know which one was talking, but I thought I heard something like "I've had enough. I've tried to be civil, but …"

My friends were at the elevator, so I hurried to catch up with them. We stopped at the ninth floor and went into the bistro. I quickly told my friends what I knew about the feud between Harold and Howard and what I had just heard. I also told them about my conversations with Howard and the conversation Jaime had had with Leonard. Matthew said, "This has gone on long enough. It ends tonight." He sounded very angry.

I definitely agreed. It had gone on long enough, but I didn't know how to end it. No one else had anything to add. We left the bistro and headed to the elevator to each go back to our apartments, walking together as far as the elevator. It would have been the perfect end to a lovely evening if we all didn't feel so shaken by the angry outburst we had heard in the dining room.

At the elevator, I said good night to my friends. Matthew mentioned that he was going to Howard's apartment to talk to him and try to put an end to this feud. Listening to the anger in his voice, I wasn't sure this was the right time for Matthew to try to mediate a feud. But I'd learned from experience that it was difficult to change Matthew's mind once he had decided to do something. Plus, I really wanted this feud to end, so if Matthew thought he could make that happen, I didn't want to try to stop him. I noticed Donna and Joan didn't try to stop him either.

It had been a beautiful evening, but between the busy day I'd had, the fresh air this evening, and the gravity of just how angry Harold and Howard were with each other, I was ready to call it a night. Luckily, Ryder was not expecting a meal. I had fed her before I went to the dining room for my dinner. Sometimes she could be very perceptive. She seemed to know I was ready for bed and didn't bother me for a treat.

As I was making sure everything was ready for tomorrow morning, I got a text from Matthew asking me to meet him in the boardroom as soon as I could. Luckily, I hadn't changed into my nightgown yet, so I was able to go immediately to the lobby. I saw Detective Handsome and his team as soon as I got out of the elevator. Darn it. I should have put fresh lipstick on and combed my hair.

Matthew was sitting outside the boardroom. I peeked inside. Howard was sitting there talking to an investigator.

I sat beside Matthew and asked him why he was there. He told me, "When I got to Howard's apartment, he and I went over to Harold's apartment. Howard had a key to the apartment and let the two of us in." Matthew had to pause before he could continue. "It looked like Harold had been strangled."

After what seemed like a long time, the investigator brought Howard out of the boardroom and took Matthew inside.

Howard came and sat beside me in Matthew's vacated seat. Detective Handsome came over to say hi to me.

I said to him, "I don't understand. I thought Harold was the wronged friend who was angry at Howard."

Howard yelled at me, "Yes, that is what Harold told everyone! And I was sick of hearing it. I couldn't take it anymore! So stay out of this or the same thing will happen to you."

Howard obviously didn't realize who the man was whom I was talking with, or else he just couldn't control his temper. Whatever the reason, he'd just made Detective Handsome's job a lot easier for this case.

Detective Handsome gave me a big smile and just said, "Thank you."

I was beaming as I made my way back to my apartment.

A ROBBERY COLD CASE

The next morning, still feeling exhilarated about last night's response from Detective Handsome, I made myself a coffee and a Danish for breakfast while I discussed my plans for the day with Ryder. Ryder did not look amused. I wasn't sure if it was my plans or my breakfast that had earned me her disapproval.

I decided that I would phone Detective Handsome with the information I had regarding the Scarborough Mechanical Belts robbery.

I typed up my notes of the information that I had learned over the past several days, hoping I had remembered it all. Then I practised what I was going to say. I learned from the bank robberies that I had tried to help with that I had to be very tactful with the dissemination of my information. I wasn't even sure myself that there was a case, but I didn't feel right keeping this information to myself. That would be a good way to approach this.

Once I had all my notes together, I got myself dressed in one of my nicest outfits. Only then did I call Detective Handsome. I briefly told him why I wanted to see him and let him know that I had some more details to share. Yay! He agreed to meet me. A good sign. He suggested we meet in the park across the road from my building. "Unless you would prefer to meet here in my office," he added.

A person's office is a good indicator of their personality, so that would have been interesting, but I wanted to meet close to home in case I needed to go back to my apartment to get more information.

I grabbed my notes and my jacket and headed over to the bench at the edge of the park across the road from our building. I hoped this meeting would go better than the last time we met here.

After approximately twenty minutes, Kevin showed up. He was carrying two coffees and a bag that looked as if it contained goodies. This meeting was already going better than the last time.

As we were drinking our coffees, I briefly explained to him what had been going on in our building recently. Of course, he was aware of that. Then I told him about the comments the residents had made to me. He thanked me for this information. It sounded sincere. I gave him my notes.

He told me that this was a really old cold case. He explained what that meant. Apparently, a cold case is an old case that is still open but has never been resolved. He seemed very excited to get some information about this case to take back to his office. He also seemed very anxious to get back to his office to talk to someone about it. I could understand. But before he left, he said, "Sara, this is an old case, but it can still be dangerous. Please be careful. I will call you with any updates." After he left, I realized I'd never gotten a goodie. Oh well, I still had half a Danish from breakfast.

I was very happy as I headed back to my apartment. I may have to put up with talk of this robbery for a little while longer, but I could see that it was finally coming to an end.

As I stepped into my apartment, I saw Ryder sitting on my table finishing off my Danish. I was in such a rush to go to the park, I hadn't put it away. She had never jumped up onto the table before. I didn't even think she could. I didn't think eating a Danish was good for a cat. Then I looked closer. She hadn't eaten more than a bite or two. So Ryder was okay. However, the pastry would have to be disposed of. But I wasn't going to let it ruin my mood. I was very happy. I was working with Detective Handsome on a case! I got out a notebook and started writing down the questions I wanted to ask. Harold and Howard were no longer here. However, there seemed to be a lot of people with a connection to this robbery.

The first person I wanted to talk to was Leonard.

I looked at my agenda for the day. This afternoon I had the games activity, which was a new activity that met in the bistro on the ninth floor. We played board games just for fun. No competition. We had met only once before, so I wasn't sure if Leonard would be there.

After making sure all my food was put away, I headed down to the dining room. I knew I would be a little early, but because I hadn't gotten any breakfast and was hungry, I looked at the lunch menu for today: pulled pork on a bun. I went in and got one. It was delicious. The carrot cake for dessert made up for not getting any goodies this morning. By the time Matthew had told us about his tour this morning and Joan had told us about the staff problems at Smith's Shoes, lunch was almost finished. I hadn't gotten a chance to tell them my exciting news. As we were finishing up our food, Karen came over to our table to say to me, "I saw you talking to that police officer this morning. Are they finally going to arrest you?"

I wasn't sure why she thought I should be arrested, so I just said no as she was walking away from the table. When lunch was over, we all left the table with a "See you at dinner."

On my way back to my apartment, Donna caught up with

me to inform me that Matthew was very upset about the murder yesterday and having been interrogated. Both Donna and I agreed that it was very upsetting to find a dead body.

Then Donna asked, "Why do you look so happy?"

I told her, "I met Detective Handsome in the park this morning. I gave him the notes I had from the robbery at that factory in Scarborough. He thought the notes might help them finally solve the case."

Donna responded, "Wow! That sounds exciting. Can I help you?"

"Yes! That would be wonderful." I added, "I have to tell you, though, Kevin said it could be dangerous."

"Why? It happened so long ago. It would be interesting to find out, but it can't ruin anyone's career now," she said, smiling.

"That's a good point. I was just repeating what I was told, but maybe the people involved don't care anymore. Let's do this! It will be fun."

Then I mentioned, "The first person I want to talk to is Leonard."

Donna seemed excited about this. She said, "Let's make sure we go to the games activity this afternoon so we can both try to talk to Leonard if he shows up. I am going to sit down to write out some questions. The games session starts soon."

I made a quick stop at my apartment to make sure Ryder was okay. She was fine, just sitting in the middle of the floor with the sun on her. Having confirmed that she was okay, I went to the ninth floor, where I met up with Donna in the bistro. Leonard didn't show up. There was a small group of six of us. We played a few different games. I won one game. Yay! I noticed that Clara was at this activity. When the leader announced that the activity was over, I realized I hadn't noticed if Donna won any games. I'm sure if she won more than one game, she would announce it at dinner.

In the meantime, we both converged on Clara, asking her if she had a moment to talk to us. She seemed very happy to have someone to talk to. I asked her to tell us about Scarborough Mechanical Belts. She started talking.

Donna asked her a few questions to try to steer the conversation towards the robbery. After about 45 minutes, I said we would help Clara get back to her apartment if she needed help. She didn't need help, but she thanked us. I wasn't sure if it was for talking with her or for ending the conversation. Donna and I headed to the lobby. On the way there I told her that Leonard hung out in the lobby quite a bit, so he might be there. I was right: Leonard was there talking with Tammy, our receptionist. I also noticed that William was there talking with Lewis. Maybe we could talk to William after we talked to Leonard.

Leonard changed his story a little from the story he had told me the other day. Donna asked him a few questions, mainly about how well Harold and Howard got along before the robbery. Leonard gave us short, quick answers, as if he were afraid of something or someone. I have to admit, I thought it was Harold and Howard he was afraid of.

Donna asked him, "Would it be better if we talked in a private room?"

"Absolutely!" Leonard answered quickly.

We wouldn't get any more information from Leonard here, so we moved on. William was still talking to Lewis, so we went over and asked if we could ask him some questions. William very rudely told us we couldn't. Then he said, "I heard the two of you talking to Leonard. I don't appreciate you stirring up this old business."

Lewis looked shocked. Donna and I both left and headed back to our apartments to prepare for dinner.

On the way there, Donna said, "Investigating is actually boring." I agreed with her.

I got to my apartment. After feeding Ryder, I headed back downstairs to the dining room. When I got there, my friends were all at the table. Dinner was beef and broccoli. I asked Matthew how his day had been. He talked about a new tour he wanted to start, namely, a walking tour of the Don Valley. I thought that seemed a little ambitious, but I didn't say anything. I knew that Bob and Doug bicycled over there, but it seemed a little far to walk. Maybe a few of the residents would do it. It was a beautiful area of Toronto.

Then Donna and I decided we would take tonight off from our investigating. During dessert, which was a bowl of fresh fruit, Donna and I discussed going to the main-floor terrace for a while this evening. Matthew was going to meet some friends in the bistro.

After we all finished dinner, we left the dining room. I was a little relieved. It still felt a bit creepy going in there. But Donna and I were going to the terrace at the back of the building. It wasn't as pretty as the south garden, but it had herbs and greenery growing there. I enjoyed being at the terrace. Getting there was not so nice, however. We had to walk past the big garbage bins and the bicycles that residents parked outside.

Once we got outside, I asked Donna what she thought of Matthew's latest tour. She laughed and said, "I could never do it." Just then, from behind me, I heard William yelling. Next, he grabbed me and threw me into one of the big garbage bins. I guess he didn't realize we had our cell phones with us. I dialed Detective Handsome right away. I thought I heard William yelling at Donna, but he couldn't find her. After a very short period of time, although it seemed very long, the police showed up. I heard Donna talking to the police, so I knew she was okay. Then, within a few minutes, the police started to talk with William. Just then, Detective Handsome showed up. I heard his voice. I banged on the inside of the Dumpster. He said to the police, "I will take him. I want him for robbery." A couple of police officers jumped into the bin and unceremoniously hoisted me out of there. I was shaking as I sat down beside Donna. When Detective Handsome finished with William and the police started to handcuff him, Kevin came over to talk to Donna and me. He explained that it was William who had stolen the money. The other two were just trying to cover up the crime so they wouldn't lose their jobs.

Detective Handsome said, "After you brought this crime to my attention, we used our forensic accountant to figure it out. We would never have been able to do that if you hadn't narrowed down the suspects." Then he added, "Great job!"

After William was taken away and the garbage bins were put back, Kevin walked with Donna and me to our apartments. We stopped at Donna's apartment first. Then on the way to my apartment, he said, "I am so glad you didn't get hurt. Having your phone with you was a good idea."

When he got to my door, he smiled as said, "See you next time. Now, take tomorrow off!"

He left as I was closing my door.

I laughed as I told Ryder, "I took this evening off, and look what happened!"

MURDER OF A RESIDENT

At dinner, Donna reminded me that the monthly Welcoming Committee was going to be meeting this evening at seven. I reluctantly left the dining room early, before my dessert. I walked across the lobby to the boardroom. No one was in there. Yay! I had finally gotten to a meeting before Karen.

Janet was there. She said, "I am so happy to be on this committee. It gives me an opportunity to meet some of the new residents as they move in."

Listening to Janet talking, I thought I should also see the good side of being on this committee. It did give me an opportunity to talk to positive, pleasant residents like Janet. I was talking with Janet when Karen came into the room, so I couldn't give her a disapproving glare.

There were a lot of new residents moving in next week, so Karen had finally assigned me a resident to welcome. My person would be moving in next Tuesday, Karen told me. Her name was Genie, and she used to work for CBC. Karen assumed Genie had been a scriptwriter there. She sounded very interesting. I couldn't wait to meet her. I left the committee in a much better mood than when the meeting had started.

The next morning, I went to the coffee klatch activity. There were only a few of us there, but the conversation was lively when I arrived. I thought I would take this opportunity to let some of the residents know about our upcoming new resident. A few of the people here had worked at CBC at some point in their careers. It was a large employer for the Toronto area. I thought they might know Genie. I asked Harry if he knew her.

Harry told me, "I knew Genie from CBC. She worked in human resources and cost me my job. It took several months for me to find another job in the same field."

I asked Janet the same question. Janet's response was less abrupt. She said very politely, "I knew her from the Art Gallery of Ontario here in downtown Toronto, or the AGO as it is usually called. Genie worked in the human resources department. I thought she was tough with the unions. I was not in a union job at the art gallery, but I heard stories from my friends."

I thought about what Janet had told me. The AGO, as Janet called it, was a government-run organization. I assumed all the jobs were unionized. But on second thought, it made sense that some would be non-union.

It was also interesting that Karen hadn't told us about Genie's career at the AGO when she was telling us about Genie. I think a number of people here would have found that very interesting. From the people in this room who knew her, I noticed a general murmur of displeasure that Genie was moving into this building. Maybe it wasn't such a good idea to have mentioned it this morning.

I personally liked human resources people and still thought Genie was probably a nice person. Human resources wouldn't be an easy job.

I noticed that Donna didn't have an opinion about Genie, Donna who usually had an opinion about the coffee klatch topics. Maybe she had never met Genie before. I was hoping

Genie would find some friends here at the Maple Leaf, some people she could sit with in the dining room or while attending the various activities here. I knew doing things with my friends enhanced my enjoyment of this community, especially at the beginning.

Later that afternoon, at the book club activity, Tom mentioned that he had heard that Genie was moving into the building. He sounded very angry. I remembered he used to work at the art gallery for a short time. While Tom was discussing his disapproval of Genie's moving into this building, his language was, let's just say, foul. His complaint didn't seem to be work-related. In fact, he never mentioned that he had worked with Genie. He did mention that he and his wife used to be friends with her and her husband.

The next Tuesday, I went to apartment 642 to welcome Genie. As the movers were moving her furniture in, I talked to her about the different activities we had here. I thought with her background, she would be particularly interested in the writing group, so I talked that one up. Genie was interested in a few of the activities, including the knitting club, which always welcomed new members. I gave her the days and times for a few different activities and told her about the monthly calendar of activities. As I assumed, she was particularly interested in the writing group. She asked for the name of the activity leader. I gave her Matilda's name and contact information. Shortly after that, I left Genie to finish her unpacking. Moving days can be very exhausting, so I gave her my contact information in case she had any other questions. I headed back to my apartment to get ready for dinner.

I had just finished feeding Ryder and was about to head out the door for my dinner when I got a text. I checked the time and realized I was a little late for dinner. Assuming it was Donna asking me where I was, I didn't check the text.

When I got down to the dining room, I noticed my friends were not there. As I sat down at our usual table, I gave my order to the waitress. Tonight's dinner was homemade beef lasagna. Not one of my favourites, but still delicious. After a few minutes of waiting for my friends, I checked my text. It was Donna advising me that the three of them were going to the Empire Pub this evening because Matthew didn't even want to be in the same room as Genie.

I thought that Matthew was entitled to his opinion, but it sounded short-sighted of him. Was he never going to eat in the dining room again? Or did he want us to change our dining time? Was that even possible? As I was pondering this, my lasagna arrived. I enjoyed it as much as I thought I would. While I was eating, I looked around the room. I saw Genie sitting with Doug.

I was glad she had found someone to sit with, but neither of them looked too happy with each other. There didn't appear to be a lot of conversation going on. I would have to check with her tomorrow.

I was enjoying my meal when Janet joined me. This was a great opportunity to find out what exactly she knew about Genie. I still didn't understand why no one seemed to like her. She seemed like a very pleasant woman to me.

Janet told me that actually some of the comments at the coffee klatch had not been very flattering towards Genie. In fact, she said some were extremely critical of both Genie's previous management style and her personality. Oh dear, it may be more difficult than I thought for Genie to make friends here. I would have considered inviting her to eat at our table, but it was already full, and Matthew had made it clear that he would not like that. I would have to think some more about who Genie could sit with in the dining room. Maybe William would be a good choice because he hadn't worked at CBC or AGO, not that I was aware of, and I think he ate a little earlier than my friends and I did. It might solve two problems. Also, William was a nice older gentleman who I didn't think had a tablemate.

The next morning, Donna, Joan and I attended a new activity here at the Maple Leaf—jewellery making. I was not good at creating things, but I wanted to give it a try. I got to the party room in good time. There was a big table we could use for our activity, so I thought there might be a lot of people attending. It sounded like a lot of fun. There were indeed a lot of people attending, including Donna, Joan, Matthew and Larry.

It was fun. We made necklaces from the beads provided by the instructor. There were several different styles and colours.

First, the instructor passed around the box of large beads. I picked a flat red square. I noticed that Janet, who was sitting across from me, picked a large green ball with dimples.

Thelma, who was sitting beside me, picked a slightly smaller gold ball that was smooth.

I looked around the table as best as I could. Everyone's main bead was different.

We had to string them on a thick plastic thread.

Next, the instructor passed around a bin holding the secondary beads. We were allowed to pick up to four of these. I noticed that Thelma picked four different beads. Janet picked four of the same type.

Next, the instructor passed around the filler beads. We could choose up to six of these. I picked six little round silver-coloured beads.

As I was stringing my beads, I looked around the room. I said to Janet, "I love this. Everyone's necklace is unique."

Janet responded with a big smile, "Not just unique. They are *very* different."

I agreed with her. Mine was red and silver. I was sure with the right outfit it would look interesting. I thought, *I am going to enjoy wearing it.* I liked the colour red and therefore had a lot of outfits that might show it off nicely.

While we were making the necklaces, we had an opportunity to talk and laugh. At the end, we all put our necklaces on and took a group photo using the instructor's phone. We all proudly took our necklaces home with us.

That evening when I got inside the dining room, I saw that Donna and Joan were sitting at our usual table. Matthew was not there.

I asked Donna if she knew where Matthew was. She didn't know. We decided to order our food without him. This evening I chose the Italian meat loaf. It looked delicious.

Donna started the conversation by asking if either of us was going to put our recently made necklaces into the Maple Leaf arts and crafts show next weekend. Donna and I agreed that we would, but Joan didn't want to put her necklace in the show. I thought that was a shame as she had made a beautifully designed necklace.

As I was finishing up my dessert, a delicious carrot cake, I realized that over the drone of the other diners talking, I heard the wind howling. I looked out the window and saw a newspaper being blown down the sidewalk. I saw the little trees across the road bending with the wind. "Wow. It's really windy out there," I told the other two at my table.

This started a discussion between our table and the table beside us about how much worse the weather was now compared to when we were children. Rather than sit and listen to this, I decided to go to my apartment. I excused myself and went straight home.

I was getting myself ready to watch my game shows with Ryder when the power went out. I was just on my way to the kitchen to get my Purdy's Chocolate survival kit from the cupboard when the power came back on. I guessed the generator kicked in as it should. I thought I would get the survival kit anyway, just in case I needed it later.

There was a knock at my door. It was Matthew. He said to me, "Shortly after you left the dining room, the police showed up. I thought you should know."

"How do you know? You weren't at dinner with us this evening," I said to him as I motioned for him to come in. "I will share my chocolates with you."

He quickly accepted.

"I showed up in the dining room shortly after you left. You will be happy to know that Joan is going to quit her job at Smith's Shoes."

He was right: I was happy that I wouldn't have to listen to her complaints about her co-workers. "Why are the police here?" I asked him as he bit into a piece of chocolate.

Once he finished his creamy piece of chocolate, he said, "I have to admit, I don't know why they are here. Let's go down to the dining room to find out."

I agreed but asked if we could stop off at the sixth floor. I wanted to let Genie know that this was not normal and everything would be okay. We got out of the elevator on the sixth floor. I saw Handsome and his team at the end of the hall. I convinced Matthew to go down there with me. Handsome stopped us when we were halfway there. "It isn't Genie, is it?" I asked. He reluctantly told me it was.

"Please go back to your apartments or I will have to question you both about your whereabouts at dinner," he said.

We each quickly went back to our respective apartments.

I would have been okay with the questioning. I had several witnesses who'd seen me in the dining room. I wasn't so sure about Matthew's whereabouts. I decided that I should pay more attention to who was in the dining room at each meal.

The next morning, I was performing my usual morning routine, which consisted of taking out the garbage. When you have a cat, this is necessary. At least I thought it was necessary. I was walking in the hallway to put my garbage down the garbage chute, still reluctant to go into the garbage room, but I needed to get rid of my waste. I quickly put my garbage down the chute and got out of that room. Then I scolded myself for being such a scaredy-cat. As I was starting down the hall to go back to my apartment, I ran into Larry. I didn't run into him literally of course. That would have been rude. He was taking his garbage out. I asked him about that because he didn't live on this floor.

Larry got angry and told me to stop interfering. I assured him that I was just making pleasant conversation with him.

Larry's reaction startled me a little. Maybe it was just being near the garbage room, but I was nervous. I decided to go to Matthew's apartment to ask him if he knew Larry.

When I got there, Donna was also there. She and Matthew were comparing the necklaces they had made the other day.

Matthew told me that he knew Larry from his short career at CBC. Apparently, they both had had short careers there. When I expressed my concern over my earlier encounter, Matthew warned me not to anger Larry with too many questions. "Genie's move-in has upset a lot of people, and Larry has an explosive temper," he said.

Matthew's answer didn't help me feel better about my encounter with Larry. I couldn't think of any reason why he would be so angry at me.

I asked Donna if she was going to the knitting club this week. We could probably talk about the Genie issue there if there still was an issue.

I went to the bistro to see if there was anyone there I could talk to. I was really hoping someone would give me information about Genie's murder. It still bothered me that Matthew, who had a very good reason to dislike Genie, didn't have an alibi for the time that Genie was murdered. Disliking someone, or the fact that someone made your work life unpleasant, was no reason for murder. I hoped it wasn't Matthew who'd done it.

Joan was in the bistro drinking some tea. Perfect. I would join her. I ordered my tea and sat down at Joan's table. We could have a nice chat while I drank my tea.

The first thing she told me was that she had heard from Doug that Genie had been strangled with one of the necklaces that was made in our recent jewellery-making class.

"The investigators told Doug that Genie had strange markings on her neck," she said in response to my question.

When she saw that I still seemed confused, she added, "Doug is assuming the marks were made from one of our necklaces.

"That sounds logical, doesn't it?" she asked.

"It does," I agreed. *Maybe I can solve this case,* I thought. "Did the investigator mention what the marks look like?" I asked her.

"No, they just said the marks were unique," she replied.

We finished drinking our tea as I thought about how to get the picture that we had taken in the jewellery-making class. If I could do that, the case would be solved.

I asked Joan if she knew what happened to the picture.

"I thought they posted it in the room where we had the class. The room is on this floor. The instructor must also have a copy on her phone," she told me.

I thanked her and let her know I was going to go find that picture.

There were several rooms here on the ninth floor. I started with the party room because it had a large table, which is why it was where the jewellery-making class was held.

I was in luck. The picture was posted on the wall in the party room. I very carefully removed the picture from the wall. The photo had been enlarged to better show off our creations. This would help me to see the exact design of each necklace, but it made it more difficult for me to discreetly take the photo back to my apartment.

I decided rolling the piece of paper would be the safest way to transport the picture. I rolled up the picture and, carrying it, headed to my apartment. When I got to my floor, there was a group outside Matthew's apartment. I went down the hall to find out if everything was okay.

He informed me that everything was fine. "We are just trying to determine who disliked Genie the most. We all used to work with her."

I didn't like the tone of this mob, so I turned to head back to my apartment. As I turned, someone mentioned the paper I was holding.

"Is that the picture of the jewellery class from the other day?" Matthew asked.

I quickened my pace and answered yes as I unlocked my door.

Once I got inside and locked my door, I phoned Detective Handsome. He answered almost right away. I took that as a good sign. I had a smile on my face as I said, "I figured out who killed Genie!"

"That's funny, so did I," he replied. He didn't sound as if he had a smile on his face. "Who do you think did it?" he asked.

"I'm actually not sure of the name. But I have the picture of us holding the necklaces we made. According to Doug, she was strangled with one of the necklaces," I admitted.

Now I heard not just a smile, but also a laugh, as he said, "Yes, that is correct. She was strangled with one of the recently made necklaces. We got a copy of the picture off the instructor's phone this morning. I was coming over soon to talk to a few people. I will stop in and talk with you. Please don't do anything to alert the suspects before I get there."

I chose to still feel good about myself. Maybe I hadn't solved the murder, but I'd come close.

Regarding his second comment: since I didn't actually know who the suspects were, I thought I should stay in my apartment and not talk to anyone. I thought this would be a good time for a tea and a cookie. So I did just that.

About an hour later, there was a knock at my door. Perfect timing, I thought. I had just about finished my tea.

When I answered the door, it wasn't Handsome. It was Larry. I stepped out into the hallway.

"Where is that piece of paper you had?" he demanded.

I started to say that I would try to find it, but I noticed his hands come up. I had to think quickly. We had learned how to avoid this in our tai chi classes. I remembered now. I swung my arm up and pushed Larry's arms away. He came back with more vengeance, pushing me. In tai chi I had learned how to stay balanced even if I was being pushed, but he pushed me so hard that I fell. I was able to get up quickly. Then, able to do my tai chi moves, I pushed Larry back one more time, but he came back even stronger. I was just barely able to keep my balance. Unsure how long I could continue this, I figured maybe I should try something else.

The next time, Larry tried to strangle me. I tried a different move, pushing him away, which also knocked him off balance. As he fell to the ground, I tried to close my door. Larry was in the way. As I was trying to do this, I saw Handsome and his team come down the hall.

He was not laughing now. "As I was trying to get to your apartment as quickly as possible, I saw that defensive move you used. It was impressive."

"I thought it was you at the door. That's why I answered it," I said as his team put handcuffs on Larry.

"Do you want me to explain what happened?" he asked with a smile on his face.

"I will tell you," I said.

"I will have to take a rain check on that. Maybe we can get together for a coffee sometime and you can tell me. I will be busy here for a while."

I guess I had offended him. I went inside my apartment and tried to get some sympathy from Ryder.

ROBBERY IN THE RHODODENDRONS

I found Matthew in the library looking for a book by his favourite author, a local author who wrote thrillers. I wanted to ask him if he had heard any rumours about Renee. He wouldn't give me any details for anything less than a beer. Luckily, we were able to buy a beer in the bistro so we wouldn't have to go all the way to the Empire Pub.

There weren't too many people in the bistro when we went in, so it was easy to talk. Apparently, according to Matthew, who hadn't heard anything about Renee having financial difficulties, said that she had accused some of the staff of stealing things from her apartment. I was glad to hear that Renee was not having financial difficulties, but I didn't like the second half of Matthew's news. It really upset me to hear. I was sure that the staff here at the Maple Leaf were very honest people who would never steal. Matthew and I agreed that she was probably just forgetting where she put things. "The things missing are socks, a book and a pen," Matthew told me. *Okay, now I feel better. This is not a legitimate accusation.* "But," he continued, "Renee's daughter is coming to help her tuck away her things."

"Oh my goodness. Now she won't be able to find anything," I said.

Matthew assured me that he had talked to the daughter himself and she was adamant that some of her mother's things had been hidden. According to the daughter, Renee had some valuable pieces of art.

The next day I was coming into the lobby on my way back from breakfast at Hockey Coffee, a local doughnut and coffee shop, and couldn't help but overhear a loud woman standing at the front desk giving Tammy a hard time. Tammy was one of the people at the concierge desk, and she was very helpful, so I wasn't sure why this visitor needed to take such a rude stance. The woman was demanding to know which apartment Renee lived in. She claimed to be Renee's daughter. Maybe this visitor didn't know that Tammy was just protecting Renee and her privacy.

Tammy phoned up and then said to the visitor that Renee would come right down. In a few minutes, Renee came into the lobby carrying a tote bag that appeared to be quite heavy. Renee's daughter relieved her mother of the tote bag and they started to walk towards the horticultural room. I got my mail and went up to my apartment after thanking Tammy for the way she had handled that situation. Back in my apartment, I did some yoga before sitting down to enjoy my tea and cookies. I also needed to get myself ready for lunch with my friends. After I got dressed, I took the elevator down to the first floor. We must have all been on the same schedule because I met up with Matthew, Donna and Joan just outside the dining room. We all arrived at the same time. The four of us sat at our usual table. Joan didn't even get a chance to start complaining about work before Donna started to talk.

Donna said, "I heard the altercation at the front desk this morning. I think Tammy should have let the woman know Renee's apartment number."

Matthew quickly jumped in to the discussion. He was adamant as he said, "Tammy had better not give my apartment number out to anyone." He then went on to tell our group about Renee's apparent valuable art in her apartment.

"How do you know about Renee's art in her apartment?" I asked him. "I don't think you have ever been in Renee's apartment," I added.

"I have my sources!" he responded quite abruptly.

This was getting to be quite a heated discussion. Frances, who was sitting at the table beside us, joined in. She mentioned that she had seen Renee and her daughter walking towards the horticultural room. I was grateful to Frances for having changed the subject. I didn't want our group to start arguing about whether we agreed with Maple Leaf's policies. Joan had to leave to go back to Smith's Shoes. Sometimes a job outside this residence was beneficial.

The next day I was waiting in the bistro for the writing group activity to start. I led this activity, so we focused on writing mysteries, as I liked reading mysteries and thrillers. I was just about to give everyone in the group the topic for this month, the topic being a seemingly nice older woman who turns out to be a mass murderer. Perhaps a bit dark, but I thought this group could handle it. Janet's story that she read last month was very intriguing. I was just about to ask if anyone wanted to read the story they had written when Glenn showed up. He told all of us, "I have a mystery. Why would someone keep a small statue that is really ugly, and then why would they bury it in a plant pot in the horticultural room?" He then proceeded to tell us that while he was waiting in the south garden for Mike to return from the Maple Leaf Espresso with their coffees, he had seen Renee and a woman he presumed was her daughter in the horticultural room burying a really ugly statue in one of the rhododendron pots. Fred was very interested in this new topic.

This bit of information put us off track for the mystery I was going to suggest we write, but this sounded like an interesting topic for a mystery, so we continued.

Janet thought maybe the statue was made out of something beneficial to plants. I thought that was a good theory.

Louise thought that maybe it was a good luck charm.

Roberta suggested it might be part of a game Renee's family was playing. She had heard that Renee's son was going to be visiting later in the week.

Frances mentioned that she had heard that Renee was trying to get rid of some things. Maybe this was how they were doing it. I thought the garbage pail would have been easier, but it was also an interesting theory.

There were a few other theories from the others. Graham said he appreciated all our input. I noticed he hadn't added any theory. I decided it was time to go back to our original mystery topic. I gave everyone the details for next month's mystery, and we confirmed our next meeting date.

After the meeting finished, Janet asked me about the seedling project that Bob and Doug were working on. I explained to her about the bumblebee project, as I called it, in the south garden. They grew flowers from seeds in small pots in the horticultural room and then transplanted them into the garden along the south end of the building, just outside the horticultural room. A number of us liked to go out there to sit and enjoy the beautiful flowers. It was a warm, sunny day, so I offered to show Janet the garden. She graciously accepted. Although one could get to this garden from the outside of the building, Janet wanted to go through the Maple Leaf and exit through the horticultural room door.

As we were passing through the horticultural room, I saw Renee in there digging up something from one of the pots. I didn't think we were allowed to use any of the pots in the horticultural room. And why would anyone want to dig up what was planted in a pot? We continued through the room and out the door into the garden. As we sat on one of the benches admiring the flowers, I noticed that Bob and Doug came into the garden. I also noticed a huge sunflower plant. It must have been more than six feet tall.

Apparently, Janet's mind was still on the confusing situation in the horticultural room as she was looking intently in through the window. She mentioned that now Renee seemed to be reburying whatever it was that she had just dug up. Bob mentioned that they came out here most days to work on their seedlings. He told us that Renee did this almost every day. "You can set your watch to it. She comes at the same time every day," Doug added. We all agreed that it was weird. Janet noted that Renee never unwrapped the package that she dug up. Bob and Doug also mentioned that she never did. She just reassured herself that something was there and then went back to her apartment.

I wasn't sure about the others, but after this discussion, I went back to my apartment to get ready for dinner. As I was preparing Ryder's dinner, I told her about the intriguing events of the afternoon. She didn't look the least bit interested. She just continued to sleep until she heard the can opener.

Going to the south garden with Janet reminded me that I really enjoyed the calm atmosphere of that garden. So the next morning, I went there for a walk before my breakfast. I did love the beautiful flowers at any time of the day. I realize that bumblebees are necessary for the environment, but I was just not a fan. I thought I could get there before the bees woke up. As I was turning the corner to head into the garden, I saw Matthew coming back from the garden wearing his knapsack. "I was just checking out a new route for a walking tour," he quickly told me. We talked about that for a while. I told him I would be very interested in this walking tour. The houses to the south of our building looked fascinating. He told me about the history of the architecture while we walked back to our building. He stayed in the lobby to talk to a few people about his idea for a new walking tour. I had to get back to my apartment to feed an angry, hungry cat.

Janet asked me if I would go for a walk with her. My hungry cat would have to wait; it was more important to orient a new resident to our neighbourhood. Janet was a fairly recent resident here at the Maple Leaf, so she wanted to get to learn more about the neighbourhood. She had been on one of Matthew's tours but found it too long. Oh good, she wasn't expecting a long walk. I didn't mind walking on the track, but Toronto, in my mind, was built on a hill. After a few difficult walks, I had come to realize why it was called uptown and downtown.

So after I had agreed to go for a walk with her, Janet and I went out the front door and headed south to the south garden. Although I loved the architecture of the homes in the neighbourhood, they couldn't beat the beauty of the flowers in the south garden. While we were going by, I thought I would just take a peek in the window to the horticultural room. Janet also looked inside. I noticed Frances was digging up a plant. I mentioned this to Janet and added that I was curious about what Frances was doing. We, of course, didn't know for sure, but Janet mentioned that Frances wanted to start some seedlings to help Doug's garden. The pot that I saw Frances holding was too large for seedlings. Then we both saw Renee. Okay, maybe Frances was helping Renee.

We decided to continue our walk. I loved the homes on the west side of our building. As we were walking, Janet pointed out another bakery. I would definitely keep this area in mind for future walks. But today, Janet and I headed back to the Maple Leaf without checking out this bakery. Both of us wanted to go to the reading group activity this morning. We got back just in time to get to the ninth floor and into the games room. We didn't usually hold the reading group activity in the games room, but the bistro was being used for the writing group.

A week later, Renee's daughter returned. I was in the lobby getting my mail when I heard both Renee and her daughter yelling at Daniel. They were shouting that a valuable piece of art was missing. The daughter threatened to phone 9-1-1. Daniel very calmly gave them the phone number for the police. Renee's daughter phoned the police. Soon Detective Handsome and his team showed up. After talking with Tammy and Renee's daughter, he determined that everyone needed to be interviewed, so they set up an interview room in the boardroom just off the main lobby.

In my opinion, the boardroom was not really set up to be an interview room for a criminal investigation. I guessed the original designers didn't realize they would need a separate investigations room. Also, there was something humiliating about sitting in the lobby waiting to be called in. It reminded me of elementary school, waiting in the hallway to be called in to the principal's office. Not that I would ever admit to having gone through that experience myself. A friend once told me how he'd felt sitting there waiting for the principal.

While I was sitting in the lobby waiting patiently for my

turn to be interviewed, I overheard Frances complain to Pamela as the former came out of the interview room that a case from her past had been brought up during the interview.

I thought I would ask Frances about this case while I was waiting for my turn. She told me, "An accountant, Thomas Little, whom I used to work for many years ago disappeared while I was employed in his office. He has never been found, and one million dollars from his business account also went missing. I won't be held responsible for something that Mr. Little did. But this issue seems to haunt me even today. This case will always haunt me," she complained.

I remembered reading about that case in all the Toronto newspapers. It couldn't have been easy for Frances. She, of course, had lost her job. The accounting firm had closed. It couldn't have been easy for her to find another job. The media was brutal to her. I tried to sound sympathetic. "Did they ever find the person who did it?" I asked.

"No! And they never will," she answered, snapping at me. Maybe it was the confused look on my face, because she added, "I'm sorry. I guess I am just very sensitive about the whole topic."

I thought I might be sensitive about that as well. It couldn't be easy with that accusation hanging over her head. When I was called in to be interviewed, I have to admit, I was relieved to get away from Frances.

I didn't recognize the person doing the interview. She was wearing a blue Toronto Police Services uniform, which highlighted her hair and eyes very nicely. She looked very young. Of course, anyone without grey hair looked young to me. She had a very slim figure. Other than overhearing Renee's daughter yelling at Daniel that day, I didn't have any information. I wanted to ask the investigator about her exercise routine, but I thought she might think that I was not taking this case seriously enough. The interview didn't last too long, so I was able to get to my jewellery-making class on time.

I picked up my mail while I was in the lobby, where I met Pamela. She and I compared flyers. Whew! We'd both gotten flyers from the same stores. I wasn't sure how I would have felt if she had gotten flyers from nicer stores than I had. No time to ponder this. I needed to head up to the bistro on the ninth floor. I got there in good time. It was just a short wait for the elevator. In the bistro, I found a seat at the table that I assumed would give me first choice of beads. I was just sitting down when Janet came in the room and sat down beside me. "I saw you talking to Frances a few minutes ago. She gives me a creepy vibe," she told me immediately upon sitting down. This shocked me. I had never heard Janet say a negative thing about any resident. However, I did have to agree with Janet. Frances had given me a creepy vibe while we were talking.

The next morning, I got to the gym extra early and took the bike that Donna usually used. Donna arrived a few minutes later. She graciously accepted the other bike. We both started to ride. Maybe I'd been wrong about this bike because it seemed to be more difficult to pedal than the other one. Could it just be that Donna was fitter than I was?

As I was pondering this, Donna spoke up to say, "Matthew is looking at buying a new computer system. He think he needs a top-of-the-line laptop."

Malcolm, who was jogging on the treadmill, joined in our conversation. He asked Donna, "Do you have Matthew's contact information? I am also thinking of buying a new computer system. Maybe he knows what the latest programs are."

I mentioned that someone must have had a sale on right now with so many people buying new computers. Malcolm's friend Harry jumped in to the conversation by reminding Malcolm that just last week Malcolm had said he was short of money and could barely afford to pay his bills.

Malcolm angrily replied to his friend, "If I need a new computer, I will have to come up with the money."

I turned to Donna and said, "Let's let them have some privacy with their argument. It looks beautiful outside. Maybe we should finish our exercises with a walk around the terrace this morning."

Donna agreed. "Yes. It's good to alter your exercise routine sometimes. And I did want to see the new herb garden Doug planted."

After we finished our walk, I texted Jaime to ask if she wanted to meet for a coffee. She texted back immediately, saying that she would meet me at the Maple Leaf Espresso. I headed right over. I joined Jaime standing in the line. After getting our coffees and maple scones, we sat down. Jaime blurted out immediately, "I'm so glad you texted me. I got a phone call from Frank. He said he recently won a lot of money and offered to buy me dinner. I wanted to ask you if Frank is gambling again."

I was unable to answer Jaime's question. Frank and I were not that close. He would never have confided in me if he was gambling, and I hadn't heard any gossip about him recently. It certainly sounded like he was, though. "Did he say how much he won?" I asked.

Jaime gave me the answer I didn't want to hear. "He didn't say exactly how much, just that it was the most money he's ever won."

I quickly changed the subject. Jaime and I both enjoyed our coffees and scones. When I finished my coffee, I remembered that I had a meditation class this morning. I quickly said my goodbyes and headed back to the Maple Leaf. Walking back, I started to think about the extra money several people seemed to have had recently. But then I thought, *No, it's probably not extra money. A person needs a computer to communicate, so if someone's computer isn't working properly, they would find the money to replace it. Now Frank, he has been trying to get Jaime to go to dinner with him for a long time. The extra money is probably just a made-up excuse.*

I got back to the Maple Leaf with just a few minutes to spare before the meditation class started. Not stopping to talk with anyone in the lobby, I went directly to the ninth floor.

There was a lot of talk about this robbery in the meditation class. I was just happy that no one had gotten hurt. I was still hoping that Renee's daughter would remember where she put the statue. I was finding out far more about my neighbours than I wanted to know.

After meditation, I had some time to stop in my apartment before I met my friends for lunch.

After changing clothes and freshening up, I met my friends in the dining room for what I knew would be a delicious lunch. On the menu today was chicken Caesar salad, one of my favourites.

"Renee has been accusing everyone of stealing her ugly statue," Matthew told us.

Everyone at the table agreed this was not possible. I didn't want to believe that someone I knew would do something like that.

We had just changed topics to our favourite subject—the staff at Smith's Shoes—when Renee stopped by our table to accuse Donna of stealing her statue. Renee started telling us, "Donna must have broken into the horticultural room in the middle of the night to get the statue."

After Renee left our table, Janet, who was sitting at the next table and had heard this, leaned over and told us that Renee was accusing everyone. "Look, now she's at William and Lewis's table accusing them," she said. I left my friends chuckling about this and headed over to William and Lewis's table. I asked Renee not to talk to Frances about this.

"It would be insensitive to mention it to her," I said.

Anjelica said she wouldn't go to Frances's apartment, but knowing Anjelica, I wasn't too sure I believed her.

I thought, *Frances will be so upset. I have to talk to her this afternoon and explain that Renee doesn't mean it when she accuses people. I don't want Frances to feel worse than she already feels about this situation.*

I soon left my friends to finish their lunch. I wanted to go back to my apartment to change my clothes before I went to meet with Frances. Even though she had given me a creepy feeling when I talked with her earlier, I didn't want to believe that she was guilty of this theft. She seemed like a nice person.

I changed my clothes, and before I left for Frances's apartment, I called Detective Handsome to tell him what I was going to do.

I felt pretty good about myself as I knocked on the door of Frances's apartment. After a few moments, she answered. She didn't look happy. I wouldn't be either if I were being accused for a crime I didn't commit.

"No one believes Renee," I said, trying to be helpful.

She said nothing, just glared at me. As she was glaring at me, I looked in her apartment and noticed a lot of very expensive furniture and electronics. I thought I should continue. "Didn't Renee come to your apartment to accuse you of stealing her statue?" I asked.

At this point, Frances few into a rage.

"No, she didn't. And you should have stayed out of it as

well," she yelled at me, starting to grab for my throat. Luckily, I had been going to tai chi for a few weeks now. In these classes, I learned how to fend off an attacker by pushing his or her arms away. Another lucky break for me was I hadn't actually gone into Frances's apartment, so I was still in the hallway.

Now, Frances grabbed my two arms and pushed me up against the opposite wall. She almost knocked the wind out of me. It was now a struggle to maintain my balance and not pass out. She started dragging me by the arm across the hall and into her apartment.

I heard the elevator door open. Detective Handsome and his team came walking down the hallway towards me. When they reached us, one of his men read Frances her rights as Kevin explained to me that, yes, Frances had stolen the statue. Because of her past, they had investigated her and found she recently sold the statue for 1.1 million dollars. Although there was a slight look of disapproval on his face as he said it, Kevin thanked me for having talked Renee out of confronting Frances. "Frances probably would have killed Renee."

I was so relieved that Renee was okay that I thought, *I will buy her a lunch.*

Handsome gave me a quick hug and said, "See you next time. Stay safe."

I couldn't wait to get back to my apartment to tell Ryder about this latest development.

MURDER BECAUSE OF A PEST

I had just walked into the reading room and was about to prepare my yoga mat for class. Class didn't actually start for another ten minutes, but I liked to arrive early to get my mat set up and get myself lowered down to the ground. It took more time than you might imagine. There were a few other people there with the same idea.

We helped each other out as much as we were able. Lucinda was there. Unfortunately, I couldn't help her out. She was too big—not fat, just too tall for me to manage. Matthew came into the room with James, who offered to help Lucinda.

While James was helping Lucinda, Matthew asked me to come out of the room with him. He had something he wanted to share with me. Luckily, I hadn't gotten myself down to the floor yet—just my mat.

So I went out into the hallway with Matthew. When we got out into the hall, he told me that Jocelyn, his next-door neighbour, had bugs in her apartment. Jocelyn lived on my floor, so I was a little concerned, but not as concerned as Matthew, who lived right beside Jocelyn. Matthew said, "The bugs could spread to my apartment." He sounded very angry as he told me this.

I was thinking, *Luckily for me, they both live at the opposite end of the hallway from me.*

"I am going to go check my apartment now. If I have bugs, I don't know what I will do," he said. I had never heard him so angry. I was sure she hadn't done this on purpose to annoy him or anyone else. Maybe she wasn't the first person with them. She could have gotten them from another apartment.

Graham lived on the other side of Jocelyn's apartment. I wondered if he was affected. Malcolm lived across the hall from her. I thought, *He should be at the Welcoming Committee meeting this evening. Maybe I will find out more then. Malcolm will definitely give his opinion about the situation, if he is aware.*

I went back into the room with Matthew. No one had taken my spot on the floor, so I started to lower myself down. The instructor was very good. It was not a huge class, so she was able to watch us to ensure we were doing the poses properly.

Unfortunately, today at the end of the class I wasn't feeling totally relaxed as I usually felt. I didn't think I felt as stressed as Matthew looked, though. I was sure we could get rid of the bugs easily, I thought naively. With that thought, I left the yoga class and went back to my apartment.

Ryder was eyeing the fish tank quite intently when I got there. So I quickly got one of her treats and put it in her bowl. I'd never had a catastrophe with the fish tank and wanted to avoid one today. I had lots of time before my next meal, so I sat down to finish what Rhonda and I called our homework. I wrote my story for the next creative writing group meeting. I was positive I didn't have any bugs and didn't want to go looking for trouble. After writing my story, I thought about Matthew's reaction to the bugs in his apartment. I did some computer research on how to eliminate bugs. It actually wasn't easy, but I was sure the building maintenance department could handle it.

On my way down to dinner, I met up with Janet in the

elevator, who lived on the seventh floor, with her apartment facing the opposite side as mine. She had a nice view of the soccer field and the skating rink. She told me that she had heard from Thelma about the bug problem on the twelfth floor. "No one from my floor has complained about bugs. And I certainly haven't seen any," she said. She then told me she had heard from Ray that Graham wasn't really sure he had them. Graham said that talking about bugs just made him itchy. Maybe that was all it was in his apartment.

I agreed with Graham. Scratching my arm, I met Donna and Joan in the dining room for dinner at our usual time. Matthew wasn't there. Donna didn't seem concerned. "Sometimes he makes dinner in his apartment," she said.

On the menu tonight was quiche. This was perfect because quiche was a quicker dish to eat. I was determined to get to the Welcoming Committee before Karen. She accused me of being late every meeting. How annoying. I quickly ate my meal, trying to enjoy the food. There was no witty conversation this evening, just complaints about bugs. Apparently, Matthew did have bugs in his apartment.

I left my friends at half past six and walked into the lobby on my way to the boardroom, where our Welcoming Committee meeting was being held. On the way through the lobby, I met up with Handsome. He quickly said to me, "This was a particularly nasty murder. Please don't get involved. I wouldn't want to see you get hurt."

By this time, he had passed me, so I turned and asked, "What happened?" But I was too late. He was already in the elevator. *Oh, I hope Matthew is not involved.*

I have to admit, after my quick discussion with Handsome, I stopped to thank the concierge for delivering my package from Indigo that afternoon. It contained the book we would be discussing at our next book club meeting.

By the time I got into the boardroom, Karen was already there. She just glared at me. It didn't matter—*Handsome cares!*

Graham didn't show up to the meeting this evening, so I couldn't get any information from him. He was probably busy cleaning up his apartment because of the bugs.

Malcolm showed up right as the meeting was about to begin and left before it was finished. I didn't get an opportunity to talk to him. I got back to my apartment and then realized Handsome mentioned that a murder had occurred here. I was so pleased to see Detective Handsome, it didn't occur to me to ask who it was that got murdered. I would have to ask around tomorrow morning.

The next morning, I went to the meditation activity. Donna had previously told me she wouldn't be there. We usually attend this activity together, but today she was going shopping in a small mall near our residence. It had a few department stores, so she was going to stock up on a few items. It also had a hardware store, so I asked her to pick me up a large pot and some potting soil. My amaryllis plant was getting out of control. I thought I needed to repot it.

Figuring I had better get back to concentrating on this meditation class, I looked around. I didn't see anyone there who would have any gossip or information to tell me. *Maybe tomorrow afternoon at our knitting group.*

In the meantime, in the afternoon, I went to the body balance exercise class. I texted Matthew to remind him about it. He liked this class. We both showed up at the same time, so we were standing near each other. As the instructor started, I heard Matthew complain to Louise that we should get rid of Jocelyn. "She started the bug problem. She should be evicted," he said in an angry tone. Although his talking was distracting me from the exercise programme, I was glad he had added that last statement. I was also happy to hear that he was talking about Jocelyn. Maybe this meant that it wasn't Jocelyn who'd been murdered. I couldn't hear what more he said, but I could tell he was still talking because his mouth was moving. This was distracting me from my exercising because I was watching this exchange. Louise just looked at Matthew like either she just didn't want anything to do with him or maybe she was afraid of him. Then, I saw out of the corner of my eye Matthew moving to talk to Lewis. I didn't hear what Matthew said, but Lewis gave him the same look and moved away. The class was almost over by this point. We were starting our stretches.

When the instructor started packing up, I went over to Matthew to ask him what the problem was. He told me he had bugs in his apartment. I took a step back and offered to go to his apartment to check it out. He declined my offer. Thank goodness. Remembering what Thelma had told Janet about where the bug problem had started, I told him I was sure that the management of the building would resolve the issue soon. "That's not the point. She shouldn't have been allowed to bring them in," Matthew said. I guessed Matthew was sure, but I wasn't so convinced that it was Jocelyn who had started the problem. I told him I would see him at dinner and went back to my apartment to get changed.

When I got back to my apartment, I had a hungry cat to deal with before I could do anything else. After feeding her, I changed out of my exercise clothes. We were permitted to wear our exercise clothes in the dining room because it wasn't a formal dining room. But I preferred to be wearing dressier clothes when I ate. Unless I was just eating in my apartment by myself.

As I was going through the doorway to the dining room, I saw my friends at our usual table. I hoped Matthew was in a better mood. As I sat down at the table, Donna started to tell us about the purchases she had made today. Donna liked to shop. She had bought a number of necessities for herself and my planter. But I was very excited to hear about all the clothes she bought. Then she told us, "I also bought a new frame." Donna's creations in our art class were really good. She picked up a few frames so she could hang up her artwork.

After a delicious dinner of ravioli in cream sauce with lemon meringue pie for dessert, I went back to my apartment. As I was sitting down with my tea to watch my game show, Donna texted me to let me know that Matthew was still upset. After I had left the table, he and Joan started complaining about these bugs. It would be upsetting to know the apartment beside yours had bugs. I was starting to almost understand Matthew's obsession about it, but he admitted that they weren't in his apartment. Joan was on the eighth floor, so I was sure it didn't affect her at all. I wasn't going to worry about this issue any more this evening. I had to think of a way to find out who was murdered. I was sure Detective Handsome would not tell me if I phoned him.

Donna texted me again: "I think you should come back to the dining room." I was intrigued enough to forgo my game shows.

When I got down to the dining room, my friends were very excited. Donna and Joan had big smiles on their faces. I didn't even have a chance to sit down before Donna said, "Joan, tell Sara what you told me."

Joan blurted out, "The police were in Jocelyn's apartment yesterday evening." She added, "I didn't hear what they said, but they carried out some things. Maybe it was about the bug issue."

"The police don't get involved in eliminating bugs," I said.

The next day, I was in my apartment rearranging my furniture to make room for the new, larger pot I had gotten for my amaryllis plant. There was a knock at the door. Thinking it might be Donna coming to help me, because I had mentioned to her what I would be doing today, I quickly answered it. It was Roberta. She excitedly told me that she had some news for me. I invited her in. When Roberta saw Ryder, she said, "Look at you. You are a very fat cat!"

I'm sure I heard Ryder growl. And as someone who considers herself slim but getting closer to pudgy every day, I had to agree.

Then Roberta said, "I'm going to call you Shnookums." I wasn't sure about Ryder, but I rolled my eyes.

I invited Roberta to sit down so we could talk. Roberta told me, "You know, I heard from Janet that Jocelyn and Malcolm spent a lot of time in each other's apartments. In fact, she said that she saw Jocelyn leaving Malcolm's apartment early one morning wearing her nightgown." She said this with a look of disapproval on her face. I was about to respond when Roberta added, "A week ago, I was listening at Jocelyn's door. I thought I heard Matthew's voice, but Malcolm came out the door. I had to quickly make up an excuse for why I was there." She giggled.

I was not amused. I couldn't even smile. Trying to give her a disapproving look, I thought, *Why was she listening at anyone's door?* I didn't ask her because I didn't really want the answer. I just hoped no one listened at my door. Of course, they would just hear me talking to Ryder.

She may have thought that she was just passing along

some juicy gossip. I definitely disagreed with her disapproval of two consenting adults' behaviour, but she had given me something to think about. I reluctantly thanked Roberta for this information and said, "I have to get back to work. I'm sure we will talk again soon." She giggled as she was walking out the door.

I made myself a tea and got a few maple cream cookies out of the box so I could sit down and think about all this.

After my tea, I had quelled my anger sufficiently enough that I felt I could go get my mail and complete a few tasks in the lobby.

I had enrolled in the travel activity for next Thursday. We were "travelling" to Africa via the computer to see some lions. After concluding that pleasant business, I picked up my mail. I noticed that Graham was in the lobby. He liked to sit there to see who showed up. He said he was just going to go to Wanda's for a Frosty. I told him I would join him. It looked like a beautiful day outside, and a walk to Wanda's would be perfect. Plus, I would have an opportunity to talk to someone whom I didn't usually talk with. Graham didn't go to many of the activities. Maybe I could use this opportunity to tell him about some of the activities that I thought might interest him.

Anita was also in the lobby. She wanted to join us. Graham quickly backed out. I couldn't blame him. Anita was always very rude to the people at Wanda's.

I walked with Anita up to Wanda's and left her sitting at an outside table while I went inside to get our burgers and fries.

We were enjoying our treat and the beautiful day when Anita told me, "Malcolm is the person who had the bugs first."

I wasn't sure where she had gotten her information or how accurate it was, so I asked her, "Who told you that?"

"Janet told me," she responded.

That was certainly interesting. I wasn't sure how Janet had found out, but she didn't usually spread untrue gossip. I would have to think about this some more.

This morning I needed to get my housework done because this afternoon the knitting group was meeting. Sometimes doing chores could be very relaxing. It gave me a chance to think as I was sweeping my floor. This morning I was thinking whether the people who had the bugs in their apartments had told the maintenance department. I was sure if they had just gone directly to the maintenance department, the issue would have been resolved immediately. Sometimes people were difficult to understand. *Oh, I promised I wouldn't get involved and now I'm thinking about it. Instead, I will think about what groceries I need. I am getting low on a few things. Maybe tomorrow I need to go grocery shopping.*

I got to the knitting group early, hoping to talk with Anita before the others arrived. It was a group of six of us who got together weekly. We all worked on our own different projects, but it was nice to get together to talk with the others. I was working on a blanket to give to the Scott Mission. Betty was working on a baby sweater for her granddaughter. I wasn't sure what the others were working on, but they all looked beautiful and a lot more complicated than my simple garter stitch blocks. Anita showed up after the gathering had started, so I wasn't able to talk to her beforehand. The jacket she was working on was light blue in colour. It was beautiful.

The next morning while drinking my coffee, I remembered we had yoga that morning. Maybe I could do my grocery shopping tomorrow. But I couldn't put off thinking about this murder. I said to Ryder, "I know I promised to stay out of this, but it doesn't make sense that Jocelyn was murdered if

Malcolm had the bugs first. Why wasn't the murderer angry at Malcolm?" Ryder didn't have an answer.

The yoga class was full. I put my mat down near Matthew and Donna. It was a good opportunity to catch up on what had been happening. Yoga was a lot more strenuous than I realized. Before I moved into this building, I had never even considered trying it. But now, I really enjoyed it. During the session, Donna kept pestering Matthew about where he had been on Tuesday evening. Matthew got up to leave. I went with him.

Out in the hallway, Matthew blurted out, "I wish Donna would stop bothering me about Tuesday evening! I think I can tell you now, but I didn't want everyone to know about it. I've started to see someone new. I met him through a mutual friend. We met on Tuesday evening for the first time. I think we really hit it off. I didn't want to say anything until I was sure about us because my last matchup was such a disaster."

I could have hugged him. Obviously, Matthew hadn't murdered Jocelyn. But then, who had? *Sara,* I reminded myself, *you promised Detective Handsome you wouldn't get involved.* This was difficult.

After yoga, I headed back to my apartment. I wanted to phone Detective Handsome. I really appreciated the speakerphone function. It allowed me to talk and write notes at the same time. He answered on the second ring. Hopefully a good sign. After I told him my concerns, he said, "Sara, I'm glad you phoned. I was just about to phone you. Do you have any information about Malcolm?" I told him everything I knew, which wasn't much. I didn't usually talk with Malcolm. He seemed like an angry, volatile man.

Then Handsome asked, "Do you have any information about Graham?" I knew a little more about Graham because he was in a few activities with me. I happily told Kevin everything I knew.

"Please stay out of this one. I know you want to try to help, but I wouldn't want anything to happen to you, Sara," he said.

"I assure you that I am trying to stay out of it," I said, disappointed that he didn't want my help.

I was just about to hang up when Kevin added, "Sara, I am starting to really care about you." He then repeated his warning that I not get involved.

We exchanged a few pleasantries and then ended the call. I was thrilled. I reminded Ryder that I didn't need her look of disapproval. She obviously had been listening in on the conversation. Then I heard a sound in the hallway outside my door. I wondered who else had been listening in on my conversations. "Oh dear, I'm starting to get paranoid. It was probably just someone walking past my door," I told Ryder.

It was time for both our dinners. One of these days I would have to be brave enough to go get my dinner before feeding Ryder. This was not the day for that. I was feeling excited about my conversation with Detective Handsome and uneasy about the noise in the hall, which had spooked me.

That evening I met my friends for dinner at our usual time. Donna and Matthew seemed to be over their disagreement. I was prepared to enjoy my spaghetti Bolognese in silence if they were not speaking to each other. But in fact, our conversation was quite animated. I wasn't sure what had put everyone in such a good mood, but I was sure I would soon find out.

"There is a new activity," Joan blurted out.

"It starts on Friday," Donna added. "It's an art class." Matthew didn't seem too impressed. I made a mental note to add myself to the list of attendees. I then started my dinner while the others talked about their day. It was such a beautiful evening, we decided to go out on the terrace after dinner. This was one of my favourite sights—the CN Tower and the city skyline at sunset. We came in after dark. I was glad I had fed Ryder before my dinner. She was sleeping on her chair when I returned. I could hear her purring—or was that snoring?

The next morning, I got up early to go grocery shopping before it got bumped to another day.

I was coming back into the building after my grocery shopping. Our driver, Steven, helped me get my groceries into the elevator, then I headed up to my floor. I had been getting low on treats for myself, but more importantly—to her, at least—I was getting low on treats for Ryder. Luckily, a quick ride to the local grocery store had resolved this issue. I still had an eerie feeling in my hallway since having talked with Roberta and hearing those sounds the other day. I quickly got myself into my apartment and locked the door. After putting my groceries away, I sat down with a cup of tea and some cookies and started a new jigsaw puzzle. As I was working on this, Detective Handsome phoned and said he would be stopping by my building sometime this afternoon. He had some names of people he wanted to question. After my tea I would definitely have to put on some nicer clothes and maybe some lipstick. I looked around and realized I would also need to tidy up here a little.

After lunch, it took me awhile, but I got things tidied up and the kitty litter changed. I put all my garbage into one bag and grabbed my phone in case Handsome called to say he was in the building. Then I headed to the garbage room. Walking back to my apartment after dumping my garbage, I was feeling pretty good. I have to admit I always felt good after taking out my garbage. I didn't like clutter.

All of a sudden, someone grabbed me from behind. He had his hands around my neck. "I told you to stay out of this, you nosey woman!" he yelled.

I tried to say that I hadn't gotten involved, but I couldn't talk. He was choking me. He was very strong. I could see stars. I felt myself getting weaker. This was really scary. His hands were getting tighter around my neck. I thought I was about to pass out, when I heard the bell of the elevator and the door opening. "Freeze!" Detective Handsome shouted as I passed out.

Later, in my apartment, Kevin explained that one of his detectives had recognized Malcolm's name. There had been a few women strangled in buildings where Malcolm used to live. "I was in the building and had finished interviewing Malcolm and Graham about this case. I guess my talking with Malcolm alerted him to the fact that he was a suspect. He wasn't aware that he was the only suspect. I was on my way to warn you. I'm so glad I didn't just go back to the office and phone you."

"So am I," I croaked.

Handsome smiled and said, "It will take a few days before your throat is healed. In the meantime, no talking.

"I'm sure Ryder will appreciate that," he said as he walked out the door.

I still didn't know if cats could growl, but I was sure Ryder just growled.

Printed in the United States
by Baker & Taylor Publisher Services